CHIPPER

CHIPPER

James Lincoln Collier

MARSHALL CAVENDISH • NEW YORK

Marshall Cavendish, 99 White Plains Road, Tarrytown, NY 10591

Library of Congress Cataloging-in-Publication Data
Collier, James Lincoln, (date)
Chipper / by James Lincoln Collier.
p. cm.
Summary: Orphaned and homeless, twelve-year-old Chipper Carey is a street-wise gang
member in 1890s New York City, until a con man introduces him to a wealthy woman
who is seeking her long-lost nephew and Chipper must decide where his
loyalties lie.
ISBN 0-7614-5084-X
[1. Orphans—Fiction. 2. Gangs—Fiction. 3. Street children—Fiction.
4. New York (N.Y.)—History—1865-1898—Fiction.] I. Title.
PZ7.C678 Ch 2001   [Fic]—dc21   00-060253

Book design by Constance Ftera
The text of this book is set in 12 point Simoncini Garamond.
Printed in the United States of America
First edition

6   5   4   3   2   1

For Abigail

One

It was nearly three o'clock in the morning. The gas lamps threw a criss-crossing maze of shadows on the sidewalk. Chipper was scared, his stomach tight, his legs watery, sweat trickling down his side despite the cool April night breeze. Pinch's plan was no good. Pinch's plans were never any good. Pinch could always see the beginning of the plan, when the gang crept through a door somewhere, and he could see the end of the plan, when they were sitting around a fire under the Brooklyn Bridge, their pockets stuffed with twenty-dollar bills. Pinch could never see the middle of the plan, where the thing got done. As a result, something always went wrong with the middle of the plan.

Rivington Street was quiet this time of night, but even so, in New York City there were always likely to be people around. From time to time somebody came down the sidewalk toward him, and occasionally a wagon rolled over the cobblestones, the clip-clop of the horses' hooves making a rhythm against the steady rumble of the iron wheel rims on the stones. A light stink of garbage from the gutters hung in the night air. Chipper tried to walk briskly, as if he were carrying a message or were delivering something, so it would appear that he was on legitimate business. The five- and six-story tenement buildings along Rivington Street were mostly dark, but here and there a window was lit like an unsleeping eye, where a baby was awake or somebody on an early shift was hastily eating a dry roll and washing it down with black coffee. You never could tell who might be watching.

This time the end of Pinch's plan was to blow a hole in the side of a bank where the safe was and run off with large sacks of ten- and twenty-dollar bills. The beginning of it was where Chipper clambered over a high wooden fence into a building site where there was supposed to be dynamite stored in a toolshed. Chipper wasn't worried about the end part, where they blew a hole in the bank, because it wouldn't get that far; and he wasn't worried about the beginning, where he clambered over the fence, for he was a good clamberer and had done things like that plenty of times before. It was the middle that had him scared. Jabber had stolen a steel bar from a pushcart on Mulberry Bend, which Chipper now carried buttoned under his worn and dirty jacket. Chipper was supposed to creep up to the toolshed, slip the steel bar through the padlock loop, and twist the lock off the hasp. Then he was to grab up an armload of dynamite, toss it over the high wooden fence, and clamber out after it.

There were a dozen things that could go wrong. Suppose the lock wouldn't twist off. Suppose there was a night watchman in there. Suppose there wasn't any dynamite in the shed. Suppose anything you wanted. Chipper had enumerated all his supposes to Pinch, but Pinch had only scoffed, saying that Chipper was just being yellow.

The building site was farther east, at the corner of Rivington and Pitt, the wood fence running about a hundred feet in either direction from the corner. Chipper had looked it over a couple of days earlier. He trudged on, huddling himself up inside his jacket as best he could against the spring night breezes that rose up to confront him every few minutes. All he could think of was being caught, maybe beaten with a club by some tough night watchman, maybe jailed, maybe both. He shuddered. He'd been whacked by cops with their billy clubs a few times. It stung plenty, but the cops weren't out to bust kids up, just run them out of some cellar or off some ferryboat where they weren't supposed to be. A night watchman might decide to bust you up, just for fun, because nobody was looking. Chipper shivered under his jacket.

At the corner of Norfolk he stopped to let a wagon rumble by. The rumble died out, and Chipper was about to cross Norfolk, when he heard the sharp wail of a startled baby suddenly awakening. A woman's voice said, "Shut the window, Charlie, the baby's cold." Chipper turned and looked up. On the third floor he could see a man in an undershirt holding a baby to his chest with one hand and patting its back with the other.

Chipper had once lived like that. Well, not with a pa— he'd never had a pa that he could remember. But he'd had a ma. He'd been six when she'd died, and he still thought about her every day. Things were always reminding him of her. He'd see a jar of hardball candy in a variety store window and remember how, if she ever had a penny left after shopping, she'd buy him penny candy. He'd pass somebody reading a book on a park bench and he'd remember her bringing home books from the library to read to him, often books about little dukes and princesses, so he'd learn how respectable people talked. He was to grow up to be respectable, she'd always said. He was better than the rest of them and wasn't to be riffraff. She was forever correcting his speech, teaching him not to say "ain't" and "it don't." "You're not like the rest of them. You have to learn to speak like respectable people."

In truth, Chipper had never seen how he was very different from the rest of them. He wore the same raggedy clothes, with his pants out at the knees, his shirts out at the elbows, his socks out at the heels, his shoes out at the toes, and all of it none too clean. Like the rest of them he stole for a living, pilfering from pushcarts, snatching purses, heisting anything from anywhere that could be sold to the junkman for a few pennies with which to buy potatoes, onions, scraps of meat for stews boiled up in lard cans.

True, he spoke better than the rest of them. At first his speech had been a source of amusement to the Midnight Rats, who decided that he talked like one of the charity ladies they sometimes came into contact with, and called him "the lady." But Chipper had got stubborn about it, because it had been important to his ma, and now that she was in Heaven he didn't want to let her down. Chipper wasn't at all sure about Heaven. He knew there was God, for sometimes when he'd done something really bad he could feel God's eyes boring holes in his back. But Heaven was stretching it—all those angels flying around among the clouds, playing harps and singing, that was stretching it. Heaven or not, Ma was out there somewhere, and Chipper didn't want to let her down by saying "ain't" and "it don't." So he'd punched a couple of kids his own age in the face when they'd teased him about it, and after a while the gang had let it go—it was just Chipper's way.

Suddenly Chipper realized that he was still standing there staring up at the man in the lighted window patting the baby on the back. He turned away and looked hastily around. A man with a dog was coming along Rivington Street toward him. Chipper trotted across Norfolk and on down Rivington, trying to look as if he had a message to deliver. The man gave him a glance but kept on going. The building site was now only two blocks away.

The funny thing about it was that they had not drawn cards to see who had to clamber over the fence into the building site. That was the usual way in the gang when something like this had to be done—draw from the greasy pack Jabber kept in his back pocket, low card had to do it. This time Pinch had simply announced that Chipper would have the honor. "Hey," Chipper had protested. "I though we were supposed to draw for it." Pinch had answered. "I decided to choose you, Chipper." Chipper had looked around at the others, who had looked away. They all had known that it wasn't right, but they had also known that if they had objected they might end up clambering over the fence in Chipper's place. It hadn't been the first time something like that had happened recently.

It puzzled Chipper. Why was Pinch picking on him?

Then ahead of him he saw the rough board fence around the building site along Pitt Street. He went on, still trying to look as if he were on an errand. The fence was about seven feet high. Chipper could jump high enough to catch hold of the top, and then swing himself over. He crossed Pitt Street and went farther along Rivington down the board fence until he came to a spot between the lamp lights where it was relatively dark. Here he stopped and knelt down as if to tie his shoe. His heart was beating quickly, and his hands felt clammy. Still bent over, he looked around. Nobody was coming. He stood, wiped his sleeve across his forehead, and examined the facades of the buildings across Rivington Street. Three or four lighted windows were scattered across the facades, but so far as Chipper could judge, nobody was looking out of them. Of course you never knew: somebody unable to sleep could be sitting by a black window, staring into the lamplit street, waiting for dawn.

Chipper backed a little way into the street to get a running start. Then he heard voices and looked around. Two young fellows were coming toward him from Pitt Street on the opposite side of Rivington. They were drunk, laughing and cursing at each other like the best of friends. Chipper began to walk briskly back toward Pitt Street. When he was well past the two young fellows he stopped, turned, and watched them until they disappeared down the block.

He turned and walked back to where he intended to make his jump. He was sweating all over now, his heart pounding, feeling weak all over. Wasn't there some way he could get out of it? Go back to the gang with some story about a watchman standing on the corner or something? They ought to have drawn cards for it, anyway. Why did he have to do what Pinch told him to do? Why couldn't he just go back, tell Pinch it wasn't fair and he wasn't going to do it?

But he wouldn't do that, and he knew why. It was because of the gang. It was one thing to face down Pinch; it was another to go against the gang. You didn't do that. Have a fight with one of them—Jabber, Annie, even his best friend, Shad—but not the whole gang. They were your blood, your skin. They were all you had.

He took one last look around. Nobody. He stepped three paces into the street, took a deep breath, charged the fence, and jumped. His hands caught the top, and in two seconds he had scrambled over and dropped onto the dark ground inside.

For a moment he crouched in the shadows of the wooden fence, breathing fast, sweating, his heart thumping inside his chest, trying to calm himself down. There was no light inside the site, no shining lantern, but from the city around came a vague yellowish glow, which lit up higher object—the top of a stack of lumber, a cement mixer, the lids on some fifty-gallon drums.

Where was the toolshed? He stared through the vague light. Finally, over toward the Pitt Street end of the site he saw a shape. That had to be it. Crouching low, he moved as quickly as he could along the fence, where it was darkest, until he reached the corner. Beyond the wall he could hear a heavy wagon rumbling along Second Avenue. Now he could see the toolshed quite clearly, a wooden structure about eight feet square, with a tin roof. He took a deep breath to calm himself. Was he really going to do this? Was he actually going to go back to the gang with his shirt full of dynamite? He would be a hero if he did. But he didn't really believe it.

He dropped to his hands and knees and scuttled forward, until he was by the side of the shed. Once again he paused to look and listen. Nothing. Nobody. It seemed odd that there was no watchman. Perhaps he was asleep. Chipper raised himself into a crouch and slipped around to the front of the shed. There was enough light so that he could see the hasp on the door with the padlock holding it shut, exactly as Pinch has said. Maybe Pinch had planned right for once. Now Chipper slipped the steel bar from under his jacket. Would it fit through the steel loop of the padlock? Holding the padlock with one hand, with the other he slid the bar through the loop. The lock rattled, and then from inside the shack came a low, long growl, followed by a short bark.

Chipper jerked the bar back, rattling the lock again. There came another bark, and another and another. Across the building site a lantern flared up. "Who's there?" a heavy voice shouted. Chipper dropped to his knees and began to scuttle toward the fence, still clinging to the steel bar as best he could. His heart pounded and his legs felt weak. The barking went on and on relentlessly. There came

the sound of running feet and a shout: "Stop or I'll shoot."
Chipper stood, charged the fence at the closest point to
him, and leaped. He opened his hands to grasp the top of
the boards and the steel bar fell away onto the dirt. He
heaved with his arms and scrambled his legs against the
fence. "Stop or I'll shoot." A light flashed on him. Driven
by terror, he flung himself over the boards and fell hard
onto the Pitt Street sidewalk.

For a moment he lay there, dazed. Then he rose to his
knees. It would take the night watchman a few minutes to
get out of the site and come around to Pitt Street, by which
time Chipper would be three blocks away and
running fast. He leaped to his feet and took a step. As he
did so something caught at his collar, pulling him back-
ward. "Hey," he shouted. Quickly he began to unbutton
his jacket to slip out of it, but before he could get the last
button undone somebody had grabbed his wrist and
twisted his arm behind him. "Stop wrigglin', yez little rat,
or I'll break yer arm off for yez."

The night watchman would be on him soon. "Please let
me go, I didn't do anything."

"I ain't found that out yet, so to put it," the voice said
from behind. To emphasize the point he gave Chipper's
arm a further twist.

"Ouch. That hurts."

"It'll hurt a lot worse'n that if yez don't fess up." Chipper
felt oddly relieved. He had expected something like this to
come out of Pinch's plan, and now that it had there was
nothing further to worry about. He would get a beating and

nothing worse, most likely. It would hurt and then he would get over it and it would be forgotten, just one more of the hard moments that came into the life of a street boy. It was a way of life, really, and he was accustomed to it. You spent a night shivering under a bridge, wrapped in newspaper, cold all over, knowing that you would just have to go on being cold until the sun rose and warmed your skin and bones. You went without food for a day, knowing that you would have to go on being hungry until you could acquire some potatoes, apples, bacon, whatever. You got sick, knowing you'd go on shaking and shivering with chills and fever until you got better. That was the way it was: All you could do was suffer through until whoever it was—God, Fate, the Devil—relented and let you alone for a while. It seemed to Chipper that it didn't really matter what form the hard moments came in. At bottom they were all the same. You just suffered through. It would be the same this time.

However, he didn't want to get a beating if he could avoid it. "I didn't do anything." He held out his hands to show that they were empty. "I didn't take anything."

"Maybe I'm just amusin' myself." Now his captor let go of Chipper's wrist and, pushing him roughly against the board fence, positioned himself so that Chipper could not dart away. He was a young man, twenty or so, and from his clothing some sort of sport—a card shark, a briber of jockeys, a confidence man swindling widows out of their tiny savings. He wore tan high-buttoned shoes slicked to a high shine, a jacket with embroidered lapels and cuffs, in his cravat what appeared to be a diamond stickpin but was probably glass. Chipper was impressed. He'd seen people dressed like that hanging around outside Bowery saloons and theaters like McGuirk's Suicide Hall and Chick Tricker's Fleabag—Fig McGerald, Googy Corcoran. Everybody feared and admired such men. Sometimes you could beg a nickel or a dime from such fellows.

"I didn't take anything," Chipper repeated.

The sport put his hands on his hips. "What was yez doin' insider there if yez wasn't up to nothing'?"

Chipper was known in the gang for being able to come up with quick excuses. "Some kid threw my cap in there yesterday. I was trying to find it."

"In the pitch dark? Come off it."

"Well, I didn't take anything."

The sport had been staring at Chipper. Now he grabbed Chipper by the chin and leaned forward to peer deep into Chipper's face. "Well now," he said softly. "Looky here."

Chipper shook his head from side to side, trying to disengage his chin. "What are you doing?" He hated having some stranger touch him like that. "Let me go."

The sport continued to hold Chipper's jaw fast, and went on staring at him. "Remarkable," he said softly. "I wouldn't of believed it if I hadn't of seen it meself."

The whole thing was making Chipper feel uneasy, as if the stranger were undressing him. He didn't like it. He gave his head a sudden jerk and broke his chin free. Then the night watchman came running up, the handle of his pistol sticking from his trouser pocket, a policeman's billy club in one hand. "Thanks for nailing him, mister," he said in a rough voice.

The sport eyed the night watchman gravely. "I wouldn't say as I nailed him, exactly, in a manner of speaking."

The night watchman reached out to take hold of Chipper. "Yez seen him come over the fence. I'll take him off yer hands." He grabbed Chipper by his collar and started to pull him away from the fence.

The sport raised his hand. "Easy there, fella. Yez got the wrong lad here. I seen another lad jump that fence, but he run off down Pitt Street. Long gone by now, I 'spect."

The night watchman looked hard at the sport. "What's yer game, mister? I seen this here kid jump that there fence with me own eyes."

The sport shook his head solemnly. "Wrong lad," he said. "This here's me little nephew Phil. A scamp he is, but he wouldn't take a dollar if it was laying on the ground waiting for him, to put it that way. He'd look around first to see who lost it. Ain't that right, Phil?"

Chipper was astonished. Miracles had been exceedingly rare in his life, and had come in small doses, on the order of a dime found in the street when he was hungry, or a warm place to sleep turning up unexpectedly on a freezing night. He knew far better than to trust it; something bad was bound to come out of it yet, which might be worse than the beating he had planned on. It made him nervous. But he could hardly start insisting that it had been him who had jumped over the building site fence. "That's right, Uncle."

"So you see, you got the wrong lad here. Phil, he wouldn't take a diamond ring if yez was to stick it on his finger."

The night watchman put one hand on his hip, conveniently near the butt of his pistol. "So yez was in on it, too? I oughta report the two of yez."

"Oh, I don't think so," the sport said. "Seein' as nobody has took nothing. Yez didn't take nothing out of that there site, did yez, Phil? Even if yez was to have gone in there lookin' for yer cap?"

"I never took a thing, Uncle." The whole thing was making Chipper feel exceedingly curious. For one thing, he didn't like uncles. His experience of them was, like his experience of miracles, slim, but the one uncle he had known had smacked him around a good deal more than Chipper had felt necessary, and he was not keen to take on another one.

"So yez might as well go back to where yez belong and mind yer own business." He put his arm around Chipper's shoulder in what appeared to be a friendly way but was actually a grip of steel. "Meanwhile, me and Phil here'll mind ours." He turned Chipper away from the fence and set off briskly along Rivington Street, still clasping Chipper in his steel grip. Behind him the watchman stood cursing. "I better not see neither of yez around here another time," he shouted in frustration. But the sport marched serenely on, with Chipper pinned tightly to his side.

Two

Now that the whole thing was over, and he had escaped a beating—so far, at least—Chipper's mind turned to the fact that he had failed in his mission and Pinch was going to be enraged, snarling and snapping at him. Pinch's faith in his own plans was boundless, and he would therefore assume that Chipper had somehow made a hash of it— lost his nerve, failed to follow Pinch's instructions. Some-day Pinch would decide, as the members of the gang invariably did, to move up into one of the grown-up gangs around, like Monk Eastman's bunch, which had, it was said, more than a thousand members and claimed the territory from the Bowery to the East River; or the the Five Pointers, which had even more members and controlled the territory to the west of the Eastmans' turf. Both of these groups took a proprietary interest in the Midnight Rats and would troll the gang for recruits as they got older. Pinch would move up someday, and somebody else would become leader.

In the meantime, Pinch was there, and it was growing clearer that he had it in for Chipper. What could he do about it? There were other kid gangs around, like the Green Devils, who claimed the area farther down the Bowery from the Midnight Rats, and whom they fought from time to time. But other gangs were the enemy and going over to them was treachery. You wouldn't be able to look yourself in the face if you did it. Besides, they wouldn't have you, anyway. Nor could you just cut yourself loose altogether. That would be like setting yourself adrift in the great, cold, empty spaces between the stars.

Chipper knew, because he'd done it once. When he was eleven and had only been in the gang for a little while, he'd found five dollars and change in a purse on the Bowery early one morning, no doubt dropped by a drunk going home shortly before. Instead of turning the purse over to the boy who had been leader—Pinch was just one of the gang then—Chipper had kept the money to himself, spending it bit by bit in secret for sweets—chocolate, biscuits, candy, stuff he hadn't even known the name of but liked the looks of. But once he'd come home from a secret eating session with a smear of chocolate on his face. Chocolate was a rare enough substance among the Midnight Rats to be noticeable, and they'd pounced. Chipper had blushed red and told an obvious lie. They had turned him upside down, shaken two dollars and sixty cents out of his pockets, and forced him to confess. After that nobody in the gang would speak to him. When they were cooking stew or grilling pork over a fire, he'd have to stand outside the circle, on the verge of tears, until the others finished their cooking. Then he'd slip up to the fire himself, cook whatever he'd been able to scavenge on his own and creep off to eat it by himself, half hidden in the shadows where nobody could see him.

Two or three times he'd decided to leave. He'd slipped off around a corner with every intention of keeping on going. But within fifteen minutes this awful black feeling would begin to soak through him, and in a couple of hours he'd feel as if he were doomed, were going to be wiped away into nothingness, and he'd slipped quietly back. Better to be at the edge of the gang, shunned, than to be all alone in the enormous empty spaces between the stars. It had been almost as bad as the time after his ma had died, when he'd felt as if something had been ripped out of his insides. In time, of course, when the gang figured he'd learned his lesson, they relented. But he never wanted to go through that again.

He had never been able to understand why it felt so bad to have your gang down on you. He had wondered if it were the same for the others, and he had watched. Sure enough, they were all mighty careful about it. Fight some other member of the gang, sure: That went on all the time. But set the whole gang against you? Watching, Chipper had seen that they backed down quick enough. Not even the leader could go against the gang.

It was a mystery. But at the moment, walking at three o'clock in the morning across Rivington Street in the general direction of his haunts around the Bowery, surrounded by tenement buildings, the stink of garbage in the streets, and the rumble of wagons over the cobblestones, clutched tightly under the arm of the sport, Chipper, at least for the moment, did not have to worry about what Pinch or the Midnight Rats thought of him.

On they walked at a brisk pace, Chipper sometimes having to trot a little to keep up with the long legs of his captor, until they had got to the Bowery, where the gangs ruled and the night watchman would not dare come in search of them. Then the sport stopped and unclasped Chipper, but kept hold of one arm, just in case. "Now listen, kid," he said. "I want to have a little talk. There's a place down aways I know of where we can get steak and eggs and a glass of hot punch. How's that suit yez?"

Suit him? Stunned, he stood in the light from the gas lamp, blinking his eyes, not quite able to grasp what was happening to him. "What?" he croaked out.

The sport laughed. "Been a long time since yez had steak and eggs, I 'spect. Can't hardly believe yer ears, to put it that way." He laughed again, obviously pleased with the effect he was having on Chipper. "Yez stick with Dick Patcher and yez'll be swimmin' in steak and eggs, in a manner of speaking."

So that was his name. Chipper remembered vaguely having heard it. Pinch liked to toss around the names of Bowery sports and sharpies, so as to suggest a wide acquaintance among these important figures, and Patcher's name had come up in this fashion. Beyond that, Chipper knew nothing about him. "Do I have to keep calling you Uncle?"

Patcher laughed. "No. We can leave off that one."

They walked on down the Bowery, even at that hour still busy. A wide avenue, it was lined with theaters, saloons, gambling houses, most of them well lit and containing customers. Doors were mostly open, and from them there fell into the street light, smoke, the sound of laughter, the thump of pianos, the shrilling of violins. The street was not as crowded as it had been earlier, but there were nonetheless people ambling—or staggering—in and out of the places of entertainment.

A few blocks farther along, Patcher led Chipper into a place called the Princess Café. Chipper had passed by it often enough in his wanderings, indeed had sometimes peered through the door, observing the men at the bar drinking their mugs of beer or helping themselves to pickles, onions, knockwurst from the lunch counter, and wishing that he could go in. Now he himself was inside, sitting at a table just as if he belonged there. Glancing around, he realized that the place was not quite as magical as it had appeared at a distance. Some of the inhabitants were distinctly shabby, their trousers and dresses wrinkled and stained. Two or three were facedown on the tables. However, at the far end of the room a piano was tinkling, two or three couples were dancing. There was a good deal of cheerful shouting and laughing cutting through the smoky air. It was magical enough for Chipper.

Dick Patcher ordered steak and eggs and two hot punches. Then he leaned back in his chair and looked at Chipper. "Yez was a very lucky lad that I come along when I done. I know that fella—he's a tough one. If he'd of got holt of yez he'd of slammed yez good. Left yez half dead I reckon." He raised his eyebrows. "I 'spect yez appreciate what I done for yez, if I can put it that way."

"I do. I do appreciate it." That was certainly true: Only

the utterly unredeemed could fail to appreciate a miracle. But Chipper's hard-earned caution was beginning to temper his awe of the miracle. Patcher, without question, was up to something. "And getting steak and eggs out of it, too. I appreciate that."

Patcher nodded judiciously. "Like I told yez, stick with Dick Patcher and yez'll be goin' in and out of the Princess like it was yer home."

Sticking with Dick Patcher, Chipper was well aware, would have its price; but everything came with a price, and Chipper was beginning to see that he might have stumbled on an opportunity to . . . what, he was not sure. Just an opportunity. "What do I have to do?"

"Aha," Patcher said. "I like that about yez. No beating about the bush, get right to it, lay it on the table, in a manner of speakin'." He put his hands together as if in prayer and stared at Chipper over the little temple of fingers. "Let's get to it, then. What was yez doin' in that there building site? And don't give me nothin' about no cap."

Chipper quickly considered. He couldn't, of course, give the gang's plans away—couldn't be telling people that they planned to blow up a bank. "They said there was a lot of stuff laying around in there."

"What stuff? There's a lot of stuff laying around every-where."

Chipper began to sweat under his shirt. He had no idea what sort of stuff was lying around in the site. "Tools. Shovels and ropes and stuff."

"What'd yez want all that junk for? Stuff like that ain't

worth heistin'. What could yez sell a shovel for?"

The sweat was now starting on his forehead. It was quite true that you couldn't get very much for an old shovel. "We needed it for . . . something."

"Who's we?"

"Us. The Midnight Rats."

Patcher frowned for a minute. "Oh. I know yer bunch. That's Pinch Mulligan's bunch."

"Yes."

"What's Pinch want all them shovels for? Dig into a bank, I wager. That's Pinch all over. Big dreams, but he don't make no sense half the time. He'll be up the river soon enough doing ten years for his big dreams, Pinch will. My advice to yez, kid, is to stay out of Pinch Mulligan's big dreams."

It was advice Chipper had already given himself, and would have gladly followed had he been able to. He was pleased to hear his judgment of Pinch corroborated by a higher authority. "Well, that's not so easy. He's head of the gang." Just then the steaks topped off with eggs arrived, giving off a trace of steam and a smell of hot meat so delicious that Chipper's mouth fell open. He snatched up his knife, but then he remembered he was not sitting around a fire under the Brooklyn Bridge eating roasted potatoes, so he picked up his fork, as well, and began sawing at the steak as his ma had taught him to.

Dick Patcher was also sawing at his steak, but he was at the same time watching Chipper intently. He shoved a knifeful of steaming steak into his mouth and, when he was chewing comfortably, said, "Somebody was teachin' yer manners. How to speak nice, too."

Chipper was always glad to talk about his ma. Indeed, he had brought her up in conversation so often with the gang that they had finally told him to shut up about her—if she was such a blame saint, where'd he come from? But it made him feel comfortable to talk about her and he pounced on the opportunity. "My ma. She taught me right. She was always on me about being respectable and such. She read me books about children princesses and dukes so I'd get the idea of it. She wouldn't let me run in the streets. She said I was better than them."

Patcher eyed him speculatively. "What did yez think of that? Bein' better than them what was running in the streets?"

"When I was little I thought it was true because she said so. When I started to run in the streets myself I saw I wasn't." He had to say that, of course; still, he wasn't sure.

Patcher nodded. "How come yez run away from home, if yez had such an upstanding ma?"

"She died. She had the consumption all along. She got it from the factory on Prince Street where she worked sewing handkerchiefs. It took her off when I was six." Suddenly the old sadness rose in him. He missed her still. He wished she would come back. He shook himself. "I had to go live with Ma's sister, Aunt Millie. She wasn't too bad, but Uncle Bert hated me. He said he never expected to have a little brat around the place sniveling and whining and he didn't want one. I didn't snivel and whine, I tried to be good, but he'd whip me anyway just for being in the same room with him. I started running the streets and got into the Midnight Rats. Around the time I was ten Uncle Bert beat me one time too often and I ran away."

Patcher nodded in his judicious manner, as if nothing were new to him. "I done the same meself, only it was me own pa who done the whipping. Richly deserved, too, to put it that way. I wasn't never happy unless I was in trouble, the worse the better. Finally he said I was gone to the devil and was setting a bad example for the littler ones. He thrun me out. Best thing that ever happened to me. Made a man of me."

Chipper had taken advantage of this rather lengthy memoir to ram home a good deal of the steak, all the while glancing up at Patcher from time to time to express interest. It was necessary now to respond and he said politely, "How old were you when he thrun—when you left?"

"Thirteen. Near grown up. Pa shouldn't of waited so long, it only spoiled me."

"I was ten," Chipper said. He was rather proud of it. There were lots of runaway kids on the streets of New York, hundreds of them so far as Chipper could see. Few of them had run off when they were ten.

"That's a little on the young side." Patcher gazed off around the room and then, in the most casual way imaginable, asked, "What about yer pa, then?" Once again he stared at Chipper.

"I never saw him. Ma wouldn't talk about him. She always told me, 'We have to forget about him, Chipper. He's gone.'

I was little and I said, 'Where'd he go, Ma?' But she wouldn't tell me. 'He's just gone. Don't you worry about him. He's gone.' That's all I know." The whole thing had always been a soreness in his mind. How come he didn't have a pa? He ought to have one like everybody else. Well, of course a lot of kids had lost their pas one way or another, but at least they'd had one for a while. In Chipper's case it was as if his father had never existed, as if his father had been wiped away, like chalk marks from a blackboard. If only his ma had told him *something* about him, anything, some little story of something he'd done, how he was kind or tall or a good boxer. Anything. But there was nothing, just a blank blackboard. Chipper felt a hollowness inside where his pa was supposed to be.

"What's the big secret?"

Chipper shrugged again. He was wondering if he dared ask for more steak and eggs, but decided he couldn't. "I don't know. Aunt Millie didn't know anything about him, either. Never laid eyes on him, she said."

Once again Dick Patcher gazed off at the dirty tin ceiling and then in the same casual way, as if the dirt on the ceiling were of more importance, asked, "Was they married? Yer ma and pa?"

"Ma always said they were. Aunt Millie, she said if they were, she was sure she hadn't been invited to the wedding. She loved Ma, she said, and took in her only child, but she didn't like being looked down upon by people who thought they were better than others."

"Who do yez call yerself after? This here aunt and uncle?"

"No. I wouldn't do that. After Ma." Perhaps Dick Patcher would buy him a piece of pie if he were cooperative. "Carey. That was Ma's name. They call me Chipper Carey."

Patcher pressed his fingertips together and looked judicious again. "This aunt and uncle yez got—yez ever go visit them?"

"No. Uncle Bert'd only whip me for running away."

"They don't know where yez is hanging around?"

"I guess they could find out if they wanted to. I don't believe Uncle Bert'd want me back."

"Where do they live?" Patcher asked.

"Over on Crosby Street."

"Yez remember the number?"

Suddenly Chipper was alarmed. "You're not going to send them after me, are you? They won't give you anything for it."

Patcher laughed. "I figured that one out for meself. Patcher ain't gonna peach on you. But I might be in a way to do a little business with them, in a manner of speaking. Never can tell about these things."

"They don't have any money."

"I figured that one out, too, Chipper. Now what's the number?"

Chipper looked across the room in the direction of the kitchen. "I wonder if they serve pie in a place like this," he said.

Dick Patcher laughed. "They might—if I was to have that address on Crosby Street."

Three

By the time Chipper parted company with Dick Patcher it was well after four in the morning. He crawled through a window into the cellar of an abandoned factory where the gang sometimes holed up, and slept until noon. He awoke hungry, but he had no appetite yet for facing Pinch. Among other things, Pinch liked to boast that until he had run away, by his own count, he had been hit at least once every day by a loving relative—father, sister, brother, uncle, distant cousin, name it. As a consequence he liked hitting people and might take a swing at Chipper. Chipper was not quite thirteen; Pinch was over fifteen and had both considerable height and weight on Chipper. The gang would not let Pinch go too far, but still, Chipper did not relish the idea of being hit.

In truth, Chipper did not see what else he could have done but flee, with a dog in the toolshed and the night watchman chasing him. But because he had tried to think of some way to get out of it, he felt as guilty as if he had actually funked it. So instead of seeking the gang out, he wandered up the Hudson River through the Tenderloin into Hell's Kitchen, trying to think of an out. But by mid-afternoon his stomach, in that annoying way it had, was snarling angrily for food. So Chipper turned his steps back downtown toward the Bowery.

The trouble was that nobody ever believed that you'd done your best if they didn't want to believe it. Chipper's Uncle Bert had first led him to this conclusion, and any number of other people had reinforced the lesson. People were not easily fooled by such evidence as inescapable facts or irrefutable logic; they also needed a wish to believe. Pinch would have little desire to believe that Chipper, with the best will in the world, could not have brought the plan off.

At nightfall he found the Midnight Rats in one of its usual dining spots, in the wagon yard behind a warehouse near the East River. They were roasting potatoes in a fire they'd made of a broken packing box. They surrounded him, greeting him with cries of "Where you been, Chipper? We thought yez was in jail, or dead or somethin'," and similar encouraging thoughts. Chipper was glad to be back among them, even though he would now have to face Pinch down.

He told the story, enlarging on it when he saw the opportunity, in hopes of creating a wave of sympathy for himself: It had been pitch black in the building site and he'd heard the rattle of skeletons dancing; there had been two dogs in there, both the size of ponies; the night watchman was eight feet tall and had begun shooting at him; and so forth, in Chipper's way of coming up with good stories.

But he elicited no wave of sympathy in Pinch Mulligan, whose face grew increasingly blacker as the tale went on.

Finally he shouted, "You should of busted open the lock like I told you and when them dogs comed out smacked them over the head with the steel bar. Whyn't cha think of that?"

"Sure." He looked around at the taut faces, all waiting to see the drama played out. "Would any of you turned those dogs loose to keep the watchman company while he shot at you?"

There was a moment of silence. "Yez was just gutless, Chipper," Pinch said. "Yez ruint it for the gang."

"I'd like to see you get that dynamite out of there, Pinch."

"Oh, I'd of done it all right. I wouldn't of been scared of no dogs."

"Well, all right, you do it then. Just try it yourself."

"Yez oughtta done it. Instead, you ruint it for the gang. We was goin' to be rich. We was goin' to have our pockets stuffed with crisp tens and twenties, stacks of them stuffed everywhere you could stuff them, armfuls of them." His eyes were gleaming, and he licked his lips. "What a feelin' that'd be, to have yer pockets stuffed with them crisp twenties, stuffed down yer shirt so thick they was stickin' out of yer collar." He began to dance a little from one foot to the next. "Can't yez feel it, boys?" He stopped dancing and glowered at Chipper. "But Chipper ruint it for us."

The gang was not responding. Each of them knew that if they accused Chipper of cowardice or disloyalty he would have the moral right to say, "All right, next time you do it." None of them wanted to challenge Chipper on that point, not after hearing about a night watchman with a pistol and dogs the size of ponies.

Pinch looked around and grunted. "Well, since Chipper ruint it for us, we gotta think of something else." He paused. "We got to lure that watchman out of there."

There was a long silence while they all pondered the idea. Then Shad said, "If somebody was to make a racket down at the other end of that there building site, it'd draw the night watchman off."

"What kind of racket?" Annie said.

Shad shrugged. "Set up a howl. Throw cans around out there." He was a pale-faced boy about Chipper's age.

"Better," Pinch said. "Start a racket *inside* the fence. Chipper'll go in there with some cans or something and start banging them around. When the night watchman goes after him, we'll go over the wall, bust into the shack, club them dogs, and heist the dynamite."

"Hold on," Chipper said loudly, "Why me? I did my turn. It's somebody else's turn."

Pinch swung his head towards Chipper. "Yez ruint the first time, yez gotta do it again. It's still yer turn till you done it right."

"That's not fair," Chipper shouted. "I didn't ruin it. Your plan wasn't any good. It's somebody else's turn." He looked around at the gang. They were uneasy, and avoided his gaze.

"See, Chipper," Pinch said. "We all agree. Yez ruint it, yez gotta do it again."

Chipper stood there, his hands on his hips, staring

grimly around at the gang. Pinch's vaulting optimism had taken wing once more. Chipper would go stumbling around in the vague light, tripping over wheelbarrows, loose timber, piles of bricks. The night watchman, who had a lantern and knew where everything was, would jump on him in five seconds and, when he saw that it was Chipper again, beat him bloody. "It won't work," he shouted. "The plan wasn't any good before and this one's worse."

There was silence. "Okay, Chipper says he ain't gonna do it. He says he's gonna get in the way of all them crisp twenty dollar bills yez was to stuff in yer pockets. He says it don't matter about the gang, he ain't gonna do it, no matter how many crisp twenties yez was gonna be flashing around." Pinch took a deep breath, flaring his nostrils. "I say he is gonna do it. I say we vote on it."

They all knew somewhere down in the shadowy places in their hearts it was unfair, that Pinch was just taking it out on Chipper. However, just as there are always two sides to any question, so there are two sides to the question of unfairness: the side that stands to gain by it, and the side that stands to lose. As is frequently the case, those who stood to gain by voting Chipper the proposed honor, grew increasingly able to see, as the seconds passed, that there might be something to Pinch's viewpoint; after all, Chipper could have clubbed the dogs with the steel bar, probably he'd lost his nerve, perhaps he'd never jumped over the fence in the first place, etc. and so forth. In the end only Annie, Shad, and Chipper voted nay, and the issue was carried seven to three.

* * *

Two or three days later, while the gang was refining its plans and gathering enough clubs to beat up two dogs the size of ponies, Dick Patcher paid a call on some people he had not known before. The apartment was on the fourth floor of a Crosby Street tenement building, overlooking a backyard strung with clotheslines over a scruffy yard into which garbage was frequently pitched for the benefit of lean, mismatched dogs that slept there in such sun as found its way down through the tenements. The apartment consisted of the two rooms: the front room, which actually looked out of the rear of the building onto the clotheslines and mismatched dogs, and a back room, which looked on nothing but the wall of the adjoining building six feet away across the airshaft. The rooms were simply furnished: a bed, a table, a couple of straight chairs, a bit of rug scavenged from a fire, an easy chair, and a sofa.

Dick Patcher was no stranger to such apartments; he had been raised in several, five or six people tumbling over each other in two rooms. Now that he had risen in affluence, Patcher resided in a boardinghouse where he had an entire eight-by-ten room to himself, as well as rights to read a newspaper or entertain friends in the common parlor on the ground floor. At present Patcher, as the guest of honor, was occupying the sofa, from which two or three springs poked up under the cloth, forcing Patcher to shift his weight from time to time in hopes of finding a space for his thin bottom between the springs. Facing him in the easy chair, which he seemed to be a part of, was Bert O'Connell, master of this domain; and consigned to a straight-backed chair at the table was Millie O'Connell.

Patcher spoke. "The boy touched me heart, Mr. O'Connell. That's the truth of it. Touched me heart. Reminded me of meself when I was his age. Now I know he wasn't nothin' but trouble to yez. Oh, that's plain as the nose on yer face, so to put it. I wasn't nothin' but trouble to me own Pa when I was his age, and he did right to thrun me out like he done. I'm shamed of it. I can see now that yez was the same yerself, Mr. O'Connell, a doting father to the lad, and he didn't offer yez nothin' for it but trouble and ingratitude."

"A truer word was never spoke," Bert O'Connell said. He was a heavyset man with a red face. He reached for a mug of beer that was sitting on the floor beside the chair. "There wasn't nothing I wouldn't of done for the boy, if I do say so meself, and all I ever got for it was lip. Lip, that's all the boy ever had to give me for what I done for him." In consolation he took a large pull at the beer.

Millie O'Connell sniffed. "It's the God's truth." She had once been pretty, but had begun to go soft around the edges, and her hair was somewhat tangled. "Bert done what he could with the boy, and if he had to chastise him now and again, why you can only say that the boy brought it on himself." She sighed. "Still, I feel bad about it. Emmy prized him so. Nothin' wasn't too good for him. Of course, she didn't have nobody else but him. She was bound and determined he'd grow up to be respectable, the way she put it. Was always on him about his manners and his speech, although where she got them ideas from I couldn't hope to tell yez. Got it from books, I reckon."

Dick Patcher nodded in his judicious way. "Yes, that's a interestin' thing. His manners. I noticed it about the boy." He gave Millie O'Connell a quick look. "Come from his father's side, I 'spect."

Now it was the O'Connells' turn to look at each other. For a moment nobody spoke. Then Bert O'Connell said, "We never knew nothing about him. Emmy wouldn't never tell us."

Dick Patcher nodded sagely. "Was they married proper? It ain't none of my business to ask, but the boy's troubled about it. It worries him. It'd ease his mind to know, in a manner of speaking."

Bert O'Connell looked at his wife. She shrugged. "She said they was. She said they went down to City Hall and tied the knot. You couldn't prove it by me. She never called herself nothin' but Mrs. Carey. Never took his name, not so as I heard."

Patcher nodded once more. And then, as he was likely to do in these cases, he looked up at the ceiling as if the subject were of the least possible consequence and said, "Of course, there'd of been a marriage certificate."

"Well, come to think of it, Emmy said there was. She said if we didn't believe her she'd show us the marriage certificate. But she never got to it."

Patcher went on staring at the ceiling. In the most off-hand way he said, "She'd of took good care of a thing like that, seeing as she valued it so much. Must of left it with her effects. Most people would." He turned his gaze to the O'Connells. "Not that it's no skin off my nose, so to put it. It would ease the boy's mind."

"She didn't leave much of what you might call effects," Bert O'Connell said. "We sold up her clothes and such after she died. Couldn't do nothin' else with them when yez think about it. Wasn't much to them. Hardly worth carting them down to Orchard Street for what they brung."

"No doubt," Patcher said. "Just one more valuable service you done the boy, getting rid of her things as soon as possible. Would of just reminded him of her constant if they was laying around." He paused and looked at the ceiling once more. "Still, she must have had that there paper stowed away somewheres. Most people would of hid it behind a drawer or in a teapot."

Bert O'Connell shook his head. "There wasn't no such thing. I don't see what's the odds. She's six years dead. It don't matter to her no more if she was married or if she wasn't." He put the beer mug to his lips as if to emphasize the point.

"No, no, yer right there, Mr. O'Connell," Patcher said hastily, fairly confident now that no marriage certificate would turn up later on to raise embarrassing questions. "It's the boy I'm here about. Now what with all the grief he caused yez, he don't have no right to ask yez to take him back. I wouldn't think of suggesting no such thing. No fair-minded man would. He's coming up to where he can look after himself. Going to be thirteen next birthday, he said. No reason for him to expect to be took back and give you more lip. But I got a soft spot for him. Can't help meself. Reminds me of meself too much. I got an idea of doing something for the lad. Not that I'm Midas with no golden touch. Do well enough for meself, but you wouldn't call me no Midas. Be a father to the boy in a manner of speaking." He studied their faces, but there was not much in them to be seen. "But I don't want to interfere. If it don't sit right with yez, why just say so and that's the end of it. Yez got yer legal rights, that's the fact of the matter."

Once more the O'Connells looked at each other, and said nothing.

Dick Patcher frowned. "Not that it's none of me business, neither, but no doubt that the boy's pore Ma given his care over to you."

"Oh, she done that all right,' Bert O'Connell said. "She given his care over to us all right."

"Down towards the end," Millie said, "when she got real sick and knew she didn't have much time left, she called me in and made me promise to care for the boy. She squeezed me hand hard as she could and looked into me face, her eyes all fierce. To this day it makes me shiver when I think of it. 'Millie,' she said, 'promise me you'll treat Chipper like he was your own. He's just a tyke, and he won't have no one but you and Bert. Promise me you'll treat him like he was your own.'" Millie looked down at the floor. "It hurts me now to think of it. She was me own sister. I just wished it hadn't of come out the way it done."

Patcher nodded. "Yes, I can see how you must feel. Too bad the boy didn't have no more gratitude than he showed."

He paused, looked at the ceiling, and in his most casual manner added, "No doubt she wrote it all down on paper and signed it proper that you was to have him. Made it all legal."

Millie shook her head. "No, she didn't do nothing like that. She didn't have the strength by then. Just made me promise."

Now Bert O'Connell was sitting up straighter in his chair, and was looking at Dick Patcher as if he had just discovered him in his living room. "What if there was?" he said. "What if there was a paper all signed and legal?"

Dick Patcher opened his hands in the most candid way. "I don't know as it'd mean nothin' at all. Might mean nothin'." He paused and frowned. "Of course, if somebody was to be a father to the boy, take him on as his own, in a manner of speaking, why, yez wouldn't want no questions asked about it later. Suppose yez was to give the boy a watch or a new hat, yez wouldn't want nobody coming along later to claim it." Patcher paused. "Yez'd want it written down and signed up legal."

Nobody said anything. The silence lay seamless in the room. Then Millie said, "Well, I don't know as—"

"Hold up there, Millie," Bert said. "Don't get hasty." He regarded Dick Patcher. "Suppose we was to sign this here paper you mention. It'd mean the boy wouldn't have no claim on us, neither?"

Dick Patcher understood the law only as it applied to lesser matters, like the usual sentence for theft, or how much a given judge had to be paid to get the sentence reduced; matters of inheritance and parental rights had never been his specialty. But Patcher did not like to allow accuracy of fact to impede a good conversation, so he said, "Yes, that's my understanding of it. Of course, I ain't trained in the law full-fledged, as you might put it, only dabbled in it, but that's how the law reads. He wouldn't have no claim on you. If, say, the boy climbed into a window where he wasn't expected and went off with a thousand dollars worth of silverware, you wouldn't have no responsibility for it. They couldn't collect one nickel from you."

Millie gasped. "You mean we've been at risk all these years? You mean that ungrateful creature could have got us sent up?"

Patcher nodded sagely. "Well now, that's a complicated point, Mrs. O'Connell, a complicated point. I've heard lawyers argue both sides of that one. But the weight of opinion, in a manner of speaking, is that it's a risk. A risk."

She looked at Bert. "Well, I never," she said in a choked voice. "After all we done for the boy."

Bert O'Connell shook his head. "I allus told you, Millie. I told you from the first day he was up to no good."

"But like I say, I'm here to take him off'n yer hands. Don't know why I do it, shouldn't ought to for all the risks that's in it, but I can't help meself. He reminds me of meself too much."

Bert O'Connell had his eyes closed and his nose in his beer mug as an aid to thought. Patcher liked to see people think in these situations, for if they followed their instincts they were likely to be right half the time, but if they thought the thing carefully through they were almost certain to be wrong except occasionally by mistake. So he waited, fairly confident he knew what to expect, and he was right.

"Now in a thing like this," Bert O'Connell said, "a man might be put to some time and trouble."

"Oh, that's understood. A fella understands that." He reached into his vest pocket and fished out a ten-dollar gold coin. He then pulled from his inside jacket pocket a single sheet of paper which had been drawn up by a lawyer, who, unlike Dick Patcher, was in fact full-fledged, along with a pen and a small bottle of ink. In that fashion did Dick Patcher acquire certain rights to the boy generally known as Chipper Carey.

Four

"The first plan didn't work, and this one isn't going to work, either," Chipper told Shad. The gang had split up, looking for targets of opportunity, and Chipper and Shad were heading for Washington Market to see what might turn up. "Pinch's plans aren't ever any good." Chipper knew that in so saying he was opening up a subject that might lead into uncharted territory. He glanced at Shad to see his reaction, but Shad did not turn his head, nor did he say anything. "That night watchman'll come after me with his club, sure as anything."

Now Shad angled his head to give Chipper a quick look. "Can't yez keep duckin' around so's he don't get a good swing at yez until we get that shed busted open?"

Chipper shook his head. "It's too dark in there. I'm bound to trip over something and he'll be on me with his club."

"Can't yez see nothing in there?"

"You can see some up off the ground. You can't see anything low down. Ducking and dodging around, I'm bound to trip." He clenched his teeth. "It isn't fair for me to have to go in there again."

"None of 'em wanted to go in there themselves," Shad said. "I voted for yez, Chipper."

"I knew you would. I figured Annie would, too. Pinch is soft on her and wouldn't have made her go in there, anyway. But the rest of them are scared to do it." He looked at Shad again. "We should have drawn cards for it in the first place. Why didn't we?"

"Pinch wanted yez to go in there." For the first time he looked Chipper square in the face. "He's got it in for yez, Chipper."

They stopped walking and faced each other. "I can see that now," Chipper said. "But why? What'd I do?"

Shad shrugged. "I heard him talking about yez with Jabber. Pinch said, 'Chipper, he's gettin' too big for his pants.' He said, 'I got to bring him down a peg.'"

Chipper put his hands on his hips and puffed out his cheeks. "What'd I do to Pinch? I didn't do anything. Why's he got it in for me?"

"What he told Jabber, 'Chipper's gettin' too big for his pants.'"

Chipper didn't understand. He was growing angry about it. It was unfair and, worse, incomprehensible. If he knew what was eating Pinch, perhaps he could make sense of it. "Shad, why does he think I'm getting too big for my pants?"

"Well," Shad paused, and moved his eyes rapidly from earth to sky, left to right. "He thinks yer tryin' to take over the Midnight Rats."

"What?" Chipper said loudly. "I never said anything like that."

"Maybe not," Shad said. "But everybody knows that someday yez will."

Chipper was struck dumb. The idea that he might become leader of the gang had never crossed his mind. Oh, he had known that eventually there would be a change of leadership—Pinch would leave, or perhaps be forced out. But in Chipper's mind that event would take place in some hazy distant time. He had never given any thought to who might replace Pinch. He stood there with his mouth open, looking into Shad's face. Shad looked down.

"Shad, I never said anything like that at all. I never even thought of it. I don't want to take over the gang. I'm not trying anything like that."

Shad looked up at Chipper again. "Everybody knows that some day yez'll take over. The whole gang knows it."

"But why me?"

"Who else would it be? Yez is the smartest one. We all figure that's the way it'll be."

Chipper shook his head vigorously. "I don't want to take over the gang," he said. Now that it had come out, he could see the truth of what Shad was saying. The gang would never accept Jabber; he was too erratic. Annie was a girl, which took care of that; and the rest were younger and would not be considered. And now a pair of rather surprising ideas began to unfold in Chipper's mind. Not only was he the best choice to be leader, but he wanted to be. Why, thus, shouldn't he be? Still, there was Shad. "It ought to be you, Shad," he said, knowing he was saying this merely out of friendship and loyalty.

Shad shook his head. "Even if I was to go for it, they'd choose you, Chipper. Yer cut out for it, Chipper, more'n

46

me. They can see it." There was a certain sadness in Shad's face and voice as he made this admission. Chipper understood that it must hurt his friend to recognize that he simply was not as good as the other boy. "Maybe we can share it, Shad," he said. But he knew in his heart that they couldn't, that when the time came he would want to run things himself.

Chipper was also beginning to understand something else. Even if he had not in any way even thought about challenging Pinch for leadership of the gang, and certainly would not have done it yet if he had thought of it, Pinch had come to see that Chipper was the threat, the shadow of the executioner coming before him around the corner. Whether Chipper knew he posed a threat to Pinch was irrelevant; what mattered was that Pinch knew it.

As soon as he saw all of this, Chipper realized that he would have to go through with Pinch's plan. If he refused to accept the outcome of the gang's vote, he could hardly expect them to back him against Pinch when the time came. His loyalty to the Midnight Rats had to be beyond doubt.

Even so, he had no wish to be clubbed half to death by the night watchman. The man was likely to break some of his bones, which Chipper assumed might be painful. Moreover, broken bones didn't always heal right and you'd limp, or hold your arm funny, for the rest of your life. Chipper had seen men like that on the Bowery. But how was he to get out of it?

When he was in a quandary, as in the present case,

Chipper had a custom of seeking out for solace and advice a sort of talisman that he had had all his life, as far as he could remember, anyway. That was a gold coin, called a Sovereign, that had the face of the English Queen Victoria on it, and some writing in Latin. It was worth some money, although Chipper did not know how much, and was dated 1849. It had a small hole drilled near one edge of it, so it could be hung from a chain or something of the sort, and carved into its surface was a large, scrolled C in some fancy script that Chipper would not have known was a C if his ma had not told him. The coin had been given to Chipper by his ma, but she couldn't remember where it had come from originally. At least that was what she had always said. In truth, Chipper believed she must have known where it had come from but for some reason wouldn't tell. In any case, he had worn it around his neck on a piece of string until he had joined the gang. Shortly after he had done so they had gone swimming in the Hudson River. The others had noticed the coin, which was clearly gold, and had taken a good deal of interest in it. The next day Chipper had found a place to hide it. He was sorry that he no longer had it hanging from his neck, where he could quickly finger it when he needed comfort; but it was nonetheless safe where he could consult it as necessary.

Now he needed to consult it, so when he got a chance later in the day, he slipped off by himself to Mulberry Street, and then along until he came to a little alley, barely wide enough for a man to push a wheelbarrow down, smelling wetly of sewers. The alley led to a brick wall that had a door in it through which a grown man could not pass upright. Chipper went down this alley and opened the door; its hinges come loose so that the door scraped along the floor as it swung wide. Inside was a small room that apparently had once been used for storage: A few bags of cement, hard as rock, were stacked in a corner, and scattered about were a lot of loose bricks. The little room had been forgotten until Chipper had discovered it. The only light came through the open door, but it had been enough for Chipper to discover a loose brick high on one wall, and behind this he had hidden his talisman.

Now he pulled the brick out, took down the coin, and held it in the palm of his hand so that the weak light flashed across it, highlighting the scrolled letter C. A feeling of comfort came over him. In truth, Chipper had never been quite sure what the coin actually did for him, if it did anything. You couldn't believe in magic when you'd gone hungry as often as Chipper had, or spent so many nights shivering yourself to sleep. Chipper would not let himself believe that the gold coin could help him out of quandaries without a good deal of effort on his own part. That was Pinch's way, to make hazy plans and hope for the best, not Chipper's. And yet, despite his determination to be smart and commonsensical about things, Chipper often went to the abandoned storage room and talked to the coin.

Now he held the coin so that it shined in the dull light, and said softly, "What am I going to do? That watchman will beat me near to death if I go over that fence again." He went on staring at Queen Victoria, and then he saw the face of Dick Patcher. Why hadn't he thought of Patcher before? Chipper wondered. He supposed it was because he had been pretty well occupied by thinking of Pinch Mulligan and the night watchman. He now realized it had been four or five days since his glorious supper with Patcher at the Princess Café. What had happened to Dick Patcher? Now that he thought of it, he was somewhat surprised that he hadn't heard anything further from him. In fact, he felt suddenly disappointed. There had been some implication that if he stuck with Dick Patcher he would . . . well, he would get something. Something desirable, that he would like a lot. Why hadn't Patcher turned up? Had Patcher forgotten the whole thing? Chipper did not think so. Patcher wouldn't have spent all that money on steak and eggs and pie for Chipper had it not been important; and if it were important, he wouldn't have forgotten it—whatever it was. Maybe he'd been busy. A fellow like Patcher was likely to have a number of irons in the fire, in a manner of speaking, and might well be busy with one thing or another. And being busy with one iron, he might have let another iron slip from his mind. Perhaps if he suddenly spotted Chipper walking along the Bowery, he would be reminded of this other iron. For it was occurring to Chipper that whatever Dick Patcher's scheme was, it did not involve his getting an arm or leg broken by the night watchman at the building site, from whom Patcher had already been at some pains to save Chipper. He put the coin back in its place behind the brick, went out of the forgotten storage room, and marched resolutely across Prince Street in the direction of the Bowery and the Princess Café.

Dick Patcher, however, was not at the Princess Café. He was instead sitting on a stone bench in a small grove of trees at the north end of Central Park. The avenues at either side of the park here were still sparsely built; indeed, shanties occupied some of the ground. There was not much foot traffic; not many children were rolling hoops or playing baseball on the grass roundabout. The few people who wandered by could not see very well into the wooded grove where Dick Patcher sat, unless they made a point of it, which none of them did.

Patcher sat with one knee pulled up under his hands, as if he was waiting, expected to wait, and didn't really mind waiting. On his lap he held a small brown-paper parcel tied up with string, about the size of an orange. From time to time Patcher sang softly to himself a popular tune of the day, "The Sidewalks of New York." Dick Patcher often thought that he should have gone on the stage. He had the voice for it, he was sure, and more important, the personality. Personality, that was the key to it. "East Side, West Side, all around the town," he sang in a slightly metallic voice. "Trip the light fantastic, London Bridge is falling down." He wasn't sure about London Bridge, but he would, he hoped, be tripping the light fantastic in the not too distant future. Suddenly he saw movement through the budding branches of the trees and stopped singing.

The woman who came into the grove of trees was in her early forties, perhaps—Patcher had never quite been able to figure it out. She was tall for a woman and carried herself with a straight back, as if she had been made to walk with a book balanced on her head in her youth. She wore a wool coat trimmed with fur against the April chill and a fur-trimmed hat to match. The garments were just a trifle youthful for a woman of her age and rather regal bearing—not so much that anyone would criticize, but enough so that careful observers, of whom Dick Patcher was one, would notice.

He stood and bowed slightly. "Glad to see yez, Miss Sibley. I hope yer well."

"As well as is to be expected," she said. "And you are well also, Mr. Patcher?"

"Oh, very well. Very well indeed." He chuckled. "Sprightly, so to put it. Full of spit and vinegar, in a manner of speaking." He was aware that Miss Sibley did not like vulgarisms and thus enjoyed sharing one with her.

However, she showed nothing on her face, but took from her coat pocket a small purse with a silver clasp. "You have brought the package?"

"Oh, I brung the package. Wouldn't do to come without the package."

She said nothing but took from the little purse some bills and held them forth. Patcher, however, did not reach for them. "I often wondered what yer coachman thinks, bringin' yez way up here to this end of the park and then taking yez back home again ten minutes later."

Miss Sibley's face grew cold. "It isn't his business to think about what I am doing or why I am doing it, Mr. Patcher. Nor is it yours."

Patcher nodded. "No doubt," he said. "But it might be if I had something to say yez might want to know."

She gave him a sharp, suspicious look. "What might that be, pray?'

Patcher waited, enjoying the moment and watching her face. He took a deep breath. "I found yer boy."

Her head jerked back an inch and her body stiffened under her coat. For a moment she said nothing, but appeared to be gaining control of herself. Finally she said, "I don't believe it."

"I didn't think yez would," he said calmly. "I figured yez wouldn't. I ain't that much of a fool, to put it that way."

She breathed sharply. "What makes you think he's . . . the boy?"

"Ah," Patcher said. "We got to go easy there, Miss Sibley." He rubbed his hands. "We don't get nothin' for nothin' in this world."

"You know it isn't a question of money." She stared into Patcher's eyes, her face as still as the surface of a frozen pond, but Patcher noticed that her hands were clutched tightly around the little purse and were kneading it as if it were a ball of dough. "Have you found the mother?"

"That much I'll tell yez. She's six years dead."

"Dead?" she paused. "Were they married?"

Patcher had already figured that it was best that they

had been married, especially as he now knew that no marriage certificate with the wrong name on it was likely to turn up. "She told people they was."

"And she told people who the husband was?"

"No. Only the boy. Too proud, I reckon. But she told the boy."

Miss Sibley thought a minute. "We never could find a marriage registered. Not in New York State, not in New Jersey, not in Connecticut."

Patcher shrugged. "They could of gone down to Delaware. Runaway couples done that. Besides, if a gent don't want a marriage registered on the books, why most court clerks'll oblige for a sawbuck."

Her body erect, her face stern, she stared at Patcher. "Do you believe there was a marriage, Mr. Patcher?"

He shrugged. "It don't matter what I believe. The boy believes it, and there ain't no evidence he's wrong, so to put it."

There was more silence. Then Miss Sibley said. "What can you tell me about him?'

"I *can* tell yez a good deal. The question is, what *will* I tell yez about the boy."

"All right, Mr. Patcher. What will you tell me about the boy?"

"This much I'll tell yer—he's the spittin' image, the very spittin' image. Looks like him to a T. To a T exact."

Miss Sibley's eyes narrowed. "I'll be the judge of that," she said. "When can I see him?"

"Soon," he said. Then he held out the package. "I don't

want to detain yez no longer. No doubt yez got things to do." So they completed their transaction.

Miss Sibley took her carriage back to a large stone house, on Fifth Avenue at Twelfth Street, where she lived. The house, which had once belonged to her parents, was four stories high, made of light gray stone, had stone balconies on the upper floors, and a round turret with a conical slate roof jutting off one side. She handed her coat and hat to the maid who greeted her at the door, and went upstairs to her room on the second floor. It was a large room, with an ample bed; ornately carved dressers; a sofa on which to lounge; some tables; walls of books; photographs of her deceased parents, along with a portrait of her grandfather Sibley, on the walls.

She took down from a shelf a small gold spoon and a Venetian wineglass with a gold rim and painted harlequins dancing around the outside. She filled the glass with water from the small sink in the corner of the room. Then, with a tiny pair of gold-handled scissors she snipped the string from the brown-paper package Dick Patcher had provided her with. Her hands were trembling now, and the paper of the package rattled and shook as she spread it open, revealing a small heap of whitish powder. She spooned some of the powder into the glass and stirred it with the gold spoon, her hands now shaking so vigorously that the spoon clinked against the glass with each turn. Tossing the spoon into the sink, Miss Sibley raised the glass with two hands to her mouth and drank off the contents in one gulp.

Then she lay down on the sofa, and soon there was

coming into her head the image of a small, bright-faced boy, laughing over his shoulder as she chased him, laughing herself, through Washington Square, the pigeons flying up like gusts of snow as they ran.

Five

Finally the moment came when Pinch decided that they had collected enough weaponry to deal with a night watchman with a pistol and two dogs the size of ponies. They had come up with three lengths of lead pipe stolen from a junk cart on Mulberry Street; a butcher's knife with three inches of point snapped off the end that somebody at Washington Market had discarded; a baseball bat with the handle broken off, also discarded; eight feet of rope, with as yet no discernable function but which might come in handy; and a supply of bricks which they had broken into chunks to make them convenient throwing size for smaller hands.

The plan, like most of Pinch's plans, was grand in outline but vague in detail. The gang would hide somewhere near the Pitt Street end of the building site—where, exactly, Pinch had not specified. Chipper, carrying two metal garbage can tops, would go down to the other end of the site, clamber over the wall, and start banging the tops together. When the others heard the watchman run shouting toward Chipper, they'd climb over the fence, force open the toolshed door, slam the dogs on their heads with the lead pipes, and carry off the dynamite. If Chipper somehow got away, or the night watchman got tired of clubbing him and came after the others, the smaller ones would drive him off with a barrage of brick fragments until the dynamite was safely over the wall. Then they'd run for it. "We'll be in and out of there in five minutes," Pinch told them, dancing from foot to foot, his eyes glowing. "It's a piece of cake."

In order to celebrate their anticipated good fortune, they had organized a feast, which they were now cooking in a fire in a vacant lot near Avenue B. The flames cast wavering shadows on their faces, on the rubbish-strewn lot, and farther back, the blank brick walls of the tenement buildings around them. They had found a sack of potatoes among the pushcarts on Mulberry Street as the crowd had thinned just before dark, discarded because they were spotted with black rot. It was easy enough to cut out the rotted spots and the potatoes were now roasting in the coals of the fire. Shortly, when the potatoes were nearly done, they would add to the coals some onions that Annie had scooped off a pushcart on Bleecker Street; and finally they would add some bacon Shad had heisted from a box set down on the sidewalk by a delivery boy who could not have lived another second had he not scratched his back up against the rough brick corners of a building and had taken so much relief from it that he had briefly closed his eyes in pleasure.

Chipper had contributed nothing to the feast. He had decided that he would be contributing enough to the evening's festivities as it was; let the others bring in the groceries. He wasn't hungry, anyway. He sat by himself a little apart from the others, feeling lonely and angry, watching them bouncing around, their eyes shining, as they smelled the hot, sweet odor of roasting potatoes and onions and thought of the heaps of crisp twenty-dollar bills soon to come their way. He felt, he supposed, somewhat like one of those Greek maidens—or was it some other people his ma had read him about?—who was showered with food, drink, and the finest clothing before she was flung down a deep well as a sacrifice to the gods.

Chipper had spent a good deal of time over the past three or four days hunting along the Bowery for Dick Patcher, peering through the door of the Princess Café at odd hours, even stepping inside to make sure Patcher wasn't half-hidden in some dark corner. Not finding Patcher there, he had wandered up and down the Bowery, peeking into saloons and theater lobbies; and when that had also failed, he had gone up and down the side streets, looking into the parlor windows of boardinghouses, identifiable because all the private houses around the Bowery took in boarders. But he hadn't found him in a boarding-house parlor.

Why hadn't he been smarter about the whole thing? Why hadn't he gotten Patcher's address, or made some sort of date with him to meet again?

The potatoes were done and beginning to burst, the soft white stuff pushing out through the skins, and the onions were getting nicely browned. Shad sliced up the bacon and handed around the greasy pieces for each person to broil on a stick to his own wishes. Now to the smell of potatoes and onions was added the strong, biting scent of bacon sizzling as the fat oozed out of it and dripped into the fire.

Then the gang became aware that somebody was standing back from the fire in the flickering shadows of the flames. They turned to look. "Mighty pleasant smell," Dick Patcher said. "Wouldn't mind a taste of it meself if I wasn't expectin' to meet with a lady who's certain to have fried oysters and boiled lobster for me, along with cold mayonnaise. Wouldn't mind it at all, except that I got to save me stomach so as to do justice to the good lady's cooking, in a manner of speaking. Who donated that there bacon?"

"What's it to you, Patcher?" Pinch said.

"Oh, nothin' at all. Just like to give credit to them noble benefactors of the human race who takes it upon themselves to see that the poor and needy doesn't go hungry."

"It come out of a delivery box," Shad said.

"Yes, no doubt. Jumped out of a delivery box of its own self. Bacon'll do that—headstrong, as you might say."

Chipper was fairly confident that Patcher had not looked in on the gang just to pass the time of day, and his heart lifted. Sitting as he was a little apart from the others, where the firelight did not so readily flash across his face, he grew worried that Patcher might not see he was there. Nonetheless, he had to be careful how he proceeded: He must certainly not let it appear that he had somehow conspired with Dick Patcher to save himself from the night watchman—which in fact he had not. He had been sitting with his legs drawn up and his arms around his knees, a position which of itself seemed to say, "I am apart from you." Now he released his knees and stretched his legs out, hoping that the movement would attract Patcher's attention.

It didn't. Patcher stepped forward into the firelight to better observe the gang. Then he said, "Where's Chipper Carey?"

Chipper did not respond, once again wary of appearing eager for Patcher's attention. "He's back there," Annie said, pointing with the stick from which her slice of bacon dangled, dripping fat onto the ground. "He's bein' grouchy, because . . ." Then she stopped and glanced quickly at Pinch.

"Ah," Patcher said. "There yez is, Chipper. I was hoping we'd of met before this."

Without looking away from Patcher, Chipper knew from their silence that the gang was focused on him intently, nosing around for the faintest suspicion of treachery. "I didn't know you were looking for me," Chipper said. That was true, more or less. He did not feel obliged to add that he had been looking for Patcher.

They were all silent, looking at Chipper. He couldn't look back at those familiar faces, pink in the flickering firelight. "What did you want from me?'

"Ah," Patcher said. "That's it right there, ain't it. That's the whole of it, in a manner of speaking." He drew from his vest pocket his gold-colored watch, which Chipper supposed was actually brass, and looked at it. "Suppose we was to meet somewheres at eleven o'clock tonight. I reckon I'll be finished with me oysters and lobster and whatever else the good lady has in mind for me by that time. Eleven o'clock, corner of Bowery and Bleecker."

Chipper had to make it abundantly clear to the gang that

he had no idea why Patcher had come for him. "What's it for?" Patcher, too, was watching him closely. Chipper wondered if he understood what was going on in his mind. "I can't," he said firmly. "Not tonight."

Pinch nodded. "That's right, Patcher. Chipper's got something he got to do tonight."

Patcher stroked his throat thoughtfully. "Wasn't nothing that could be put off, was it Pinch? Nothing that couldn't wait a day?"

"No," Pinch said. "It can't be put off."

Patcher stroked his throat again and said, "Hmmm." Then he said, "Yez wasn't planning to send Chipper back into that there building site, was yez, Pinch? That couldn't be it, not by any little chance?"

Nobody said anything. Then Pinch said, "So what if it was?"

"Aha." Patcher put the watch back in his vest pocket and slid his right hand casually into his jacket pocket, where in the flickering light it made a rather large lump. "Now I'll tell yez the so what of it, Pinch. I got other uses for Chipper, which don't call for him gettin' his face busted up by no night watchman. No, Chipper gettin' his nose bent and his eyes turned slanchwise ain't in my plans, to put it that way." He paused. "So now that we understand each other like gentlemen, I expect to see Chipper at Bowery and Bleecker at eleven o'clock."

Somewhere during this last remark Pinch had stood and was facing Patcher, about ten feet away. Patcher was some five years older than Pinch, and a good six inches taller, but

Pinch had the gang behind him. Still, there was the question of what Patcher might be gripping in his right-hand jacket pocket. "Patcher, Chipper said he ain't free tonight. That oughtta be good enough right there."

Patcher moved so fast nobody could stop him. One moment he was standing calmly five feet from the fire; the next moment he had Pinch's arm twisted behind his back and the muzzle of a small steel pistol pressed hard into the back of Pinch's neck. "I'm tellin' yez, Pinch," he said in a voice tight with rage, "if Chipper ain't where I said tonight, I'm gonna murder yez, sure as yez got a nose on yer face, which yez won't when I get finished with yez. And that ain't no manner of speakin', neither." He jabbed the muzzle of the pistol hard into the muscles of Pinch's neck, making him squeal. Then he shoved Pinch onto the dirt by the fire and strode away into the flickering gloom of the vacant lot.

Pinch scrambled to his feet. "I'm gonna getcha, Patcher," he screamed into the night. "I'm gonna getcha if it takes me the rest of me life." Patcher did not turn, but stuck a finger high into the air behind him.

It took Chipper the best part of two days to persuade the gang that he wasn't up to anything with Patcher. His best chance, he knew, was to bring Shad around, for Shad would give him the benefit of the doubt and might go from there to convince the others. "I don't know what it's all about," he told Shad the next morning when they had a chance to talk. "He wants me to deliver a bunch of flowers to some lady up on Fifth Avenue. That's all he wants. It's just a delivery."

Shad frowned. "It's an awful lot of fuss for a delivery."

Chipper shook his head. "I can't help it. It's the truth. That's all he told me. He wants me to deliver some flowers to this lady up on Fifth Avenue."

"There's got to be something behind it," Shad said.

Later on, when Pinch got in on the conversation he said, "She's some rich old lady and Patcher's planning a heist at her place. That's gotta be it. It don't make sense otherwise. Yez gotta let us in on it, Carey. Yez double-crossed us once already, yez better not double-cross us again."

"How did I double-cross you, Pinch? I didn't."

"Yez was cookin' up something with Patcher and wasn't gonna let us in on it. Well, you better."

But in the end, they came around, to a degree at least. It looked suspicious all right, but on the other hand they had known Chipper for a long time—had snatched purses with him, slept heaped up with him in cellars, and all the rest of it. They knew his flesh, knew his way of thinking; he was one of them, and they could not really believe that he would double-cross them. That wasn't Chipper. The Chipper they knew did right by the gang—shared, comforted the younger ones when they were scared or lonely, saw to it that someone shivering with chills and fever had water and something to cover him at night. He wouldn't double-cross them. Still, even Chipper had to admit that it looked suspicious.

"Look," he said, "if anyone's up to something, it's

Patcher, not me. I told you what he wants me to do. If you don't believe me, come and see for yourself."

"Oh, we're gonna do that, Chipper," Pinch said. "We're gonna see for ourselfs."

On the Wednesday following, Chipper went to a particular florist's shop on Fifth Avenue that Patcher had indicated. Here Chipper picked up a bouquet of flowers to be delivered to a Miss Sibley at an address on Fifth Avenue written on a slip of paper attached to the flowers. The flowers were worth a good deal, apparently. "They cost a pretty penny, be careful how you handle them," the florist said.

Chipper knew that flowers could be expensive. He had not had much experience with them, as his environment was not much noted for its natural beauty, but there had sometimes been flowers in old St. Patrick's on Mulberry Street when he had gone—his ma had always said that respectable people went to church on Sunday. Chipper had wanted flowers for his ma's funeral, and he had asked Aunt Millie about it, but she had said there was no money for such things. As Chipper walked up Fifth Avenue, with its wide sidewalks and pretty carriages flowing past the handsome houses, with here and there a church steeple pointing skyward above the rooftops, he was thinking about his ma. He wondered if she was looking down on him now from wherever she was, seeing him marching up Fifth Avenue carrying a large bouquet of flowers. He began to pretend that he was carrying them to her somewhere, and how she would clap her hands together and say, "Chipper, how beautiful, where did you get them?" or something like that, at any rate. But as he came close to the specified address, he had to stop daydreaming. He wondered: Would they miss a couple of flowers if he stole them to put on his mother's grave? If he could still find it. Aunt Millie used to take him out to it on Easter, so they could clear the dead leaves off it; but that had been a while ago. Besides, they'd probably notice if he stole some flowers.

Now he turned his head to take a quick glance over his shoulder. He could see Shad and Pinch loitering along a couple of blocks behind him. He looked around, trying to find a clock: Patcher had told him to arrive promptly at ten o'clock. Ahead he saw a jeweler's shop. There would be watches in the window and, he presumed, a clock. There was: five minutes of ten. He slowed his pace slightly, checking the street numbers, and picked out the house he wanted. It was indeed grand, the sort of place that could provide a proper setting for so gorgeous a bouquet of flowers, he figured. He still had a minute or two to kill, and he paused to inspect the house. With its stone-balustraded balconies on the upper floors and the round turret with its conical roof, it reminded him of palaces he had seen in pictures in the King Arthur book his ma had read to him. The turret was specially interesting. Was the room inside also round? He imagined that it was. It would be a lot of fun to live in a round room in a turret. You could pretend you were Merlin or something, shooting magical lightning bolts out at enemy knights.

The front door was reached by a flight of steps with iron

scrollwork banisters up the sides. On either side of the door itself were large stained-glass windows showing cranes in marshy places. For a moment Chipper stood there admiring the way the light from inside the house brightened the colors of the stained glass. Between the flowers and the glass, it was almost like being in church. Perhaps he ought to start going to church again, although he'd have to lie about it to the gang. Would they let street boys into church, do you suppose?

Chipper was, of course, unaware that standing just behind a curtain hanging in a window near the front door was the intended recipient of the flowers, Miss Sibley. In her hand she held a scrawled and somewhat smudged note which read, "A boy will delver flors at 10 AM Wensdy prompt. Catch a look at him. Your friend Dick Patcher.

From her vantage point somewhat above the street, she saw a boy of about twelve, coming along the sidewalk with a bundle of flowers. Beneath her long gray dress she was trembling, her heart thumping so loud it beat in her ears. She said to herself, "I'm acting like a silly girl, I must pull myself together, I mustn't give way to my feelings. It can't really be him. It can't be the right boy. It's a confidence scheme of Patcher's. The boy won't be anything like him. I must get over this." But all the same she was praying it would be he.

The boy now paused a few paces away from the steps, apparently checking the number of the house. The bundle was large and covered a good deal of his face. The dark brown hair was the same as in the portrait, but of course that could have been dyed. The boy was a ragamuffin, that, too, was clear. There was a hole in one knee of his pants and a patch on the other knee. He wore a red sweater that was out at both elbows, a dirty cloth cap, badly worn shoes, and socks that drooped loosely around the tops of the shoes.

Now the boy started walking toward the steps. At this angle she could see more of his face. Perhaps there was a resemblance, she thought, and her heart skipped. "I mustn't get carried away,' she cautioned herself. "It's a confidence game."

The boy mounted the steps and disappeared from her view. Suddenly the bell pealed. She jumped as if she had received an electric shock. Immediately a maid in a white apron appeared, heading for the door. "No, Amanda," Miss Sibley said. "I'll get it myself. I'm expecting something." She looked at her watch: ten o'clock exactly. She went to the door, and taking a deep breath, she pulled it open.

The boy was a step below her, and when he held the flowers out to her, they entirely obscured his face. "I was told to deliver these, Ma'am." His voice was achingly familiar, and her hands began to shake. She took the bundle, and there before her was that face. Not the same exactly; not quite the face in the portrait. But it was familiar, oh so familiar. She had an eerie sensation, as if the world were spinning, and for a moment she felt detached from everything, her mind blank.

"Are you all right, Ma'am?"

Miss Sibley realized that she had gone white and was clutching the doorjamb. "Yes, yes," she gasped. She straightened herself. "I'm all right." Holding the large bundle of flowers under her arm, she fumbled open the small purse with the silver clasp, dipped her hand blindly into the purse, pulled out a dollar to hand to Chipper. He gasped: It was rare to have that much money for himself. He turned and ran down the steps.

Miss Sibley stepped back inside the house, closed the door, dropped the flowers to the floor, and stood with her hands over her face, tears cascading through her fingers. "I'm behaving like a silly girl," she told herself. "I can't let the servants see me like this. I must stop it. It's a confidence game." Then she picked up the flowers, went upstairs to her room, and feverishly mixed herself a draught of her white powders.

Pinch and Shad were waiting for Chipper a couple of blocks down Fifth Avenue. When he came up to them, he said, "See, I told you there wasn't anything to it. Patcher just wanted someone to deliver those flowers." Chipper knew, however, that this wasn't true. Why had the woman nearly fainted when he handed her the flowers? Was she in love with Dick Patcher? That seemed improbable even to Chipper, who didn't know much about being in love.

"Wasn't nothin' to it, Chipper?" Pinch said. "Them people, they're millionaires. Who'd yez give the flowers to?"

Chipper was feeling a lot more comfortable than he had earlier. Nothing had come out of it that could make the gang worry about him. "Some old lady. Well, maybe not so old. I don't know how old she was."

"Did she have on a lot of jewels—pearl necklaces and diamond rings?"

Chipper thought a moment. "I didn't notice," he said finally.

"Yez didn't notice? That was the most important thing."

"She was holding the flowers up in front of her. I couldn't see if she had a necklace on or what."

Slowly Chipper reached into his pocket and drew forth the dollar bill. "She gave me a dollar."

Pinch and Shad gasped as one. "A dollar?"

Chipper handed the bill to Pinch. "See?" Shad said. "I told yez, Pinch, Chipper wasn't up to nothin'. He's givin' the dollar over to the gang."

Pinch frowned. "Well, all right,' he said. "Still, Patcher's worming his way in there, buttering that old lady up with flowers and such. Patcher ain't sendin' no flowers to no old lady for nothin'. He's working his way in there. He's gonna clean the place out. Yez gotta get us in on it, Chipper. We gotta get our share."

Pinch was once again digging his teeth into an idea without thinking it through very clearly. Just as he had seen heaps of twenty-dollar bills and had fixed his mind on the dynamite he had supposed was in the building site, so he was seeing heaps of gold and diamond jewelry and was fixing his mind on getting into the grand house on Fifth Avenue. Chipper could see that Pinch was going to put him in the middle once again. He wished Pinch would just once listen to reason. "Pinch, leave me alone, will you? Do you think Patcher's going to spill all his plans to me? Why's he going to let me in on it? How'm I going to do anything about it?"

There was something in that, and they wandered on back down Fifth Avenue in a more lighthearted mood. Chipper saw that, for the moment at least, he was back in the good graces of the gang. But he was also fairly sure that Dick Patcher was not planning anything so simple as robbing that grand house.

Six

That afternoon Dick Patcher and Elizabeth Sibley met once again by the stone bench in the grove of trees at the north end of Central Park. Miss Sibley had, through strength of character, composed her mind. She had sent a note to the family lawyer, William Hodge, Esq., who was also her second cousin, that she wished to see him in his office two days hence. She was three years older than William; but she had never quite got over seeing him as merely a younger cousin. Still, he knew the family secrets: That was important. She mentioned none of this to Dick Patcher.

"I grant you," she said, her voice firm and clear, "he's very like. I admit to having been startled by the likeness. Not a twin, certainly; but the resemblance is clear."

"I told yez," Patcher said. "I wouldn't steer yez wrong. I knew it was him the minute I laid eyes on him."

Miss Sibley shook her head calmly but decisively. "I didn't say it was he, Mr. Patcher. I merely said that he was very like."

"He's well spoke, too, as the sayin' is. He was trained proper by someone. Got some manners."

"Anyone can learn to speak well if they put their mind to it—and have sufficient reason for doing so."

"Not from me they wouldn't. I couldn't never teach nobody how to be well spoke."

Miss Sibley stared at Patcher. "I wasn't suggesting that you could." She paused. "It could all be sheer coincidence. We frequently meet people who resemble others."

"Not so close as this. Not this close."

She closed her eyes, once again seeing the laughing boy chasing pigeons in Washington Square. "I'll grant he is very like." There was a little silence. "What, then, do you propose, Mr. Patcher?"

He tipped his head and gave her a look. "I was thinkin' it was up to yez to propose, if I can put it that way."

"What have you said to the boy?"

"Nothin'. We ain't got that far along in this here thing yet. You and me ain't reached no understandin' yet, so to speak."

"What proof can you give me?"

"Why don't yez talk to the boy yerself?"

Once more she closed her eyes. Oh, she wanted to do that very much. She wanted to look into that face, hear that voice, and find there the laughing boy she had chased around Washington Square so many times. But she was afraid. That it might be some sort of a confidence game did not worry her. That might be the case even if he were the boy. She believed she could protect herself against something like that. She had always taken risks and didn't mind gambling. Nor was she terribly worried that she would discover soon enough that he wasn't the boy. So much the better, really. It would be over and she could get on with her life. It might be for the best that way. No, the real worry was that he might in fact turn out to be the boy after all. The odds were, of course, long; but long shots sometimes paid off. Then what? What would she do then? That might be the most difficult thing.

But she wanted it. "I'll talk to the boy," she said. "Bring him to this address." She took from her coat pocket the stub of a pencil and on the back of her calling card wrote the address of her cousin William Hodge's office. "Three-thirty on Friday. Please be prompt. I don't like to be kept waiting."

It was just as Chipper had feared: Pinch Mulligan had now got his mind set on the grand house on Fifth Avenue, with what he supposed were heaps of pearls, diamonds, gold, silver, lying around on tables and in dishes waiting for some ambitious young person to scoop them up. This new adventure had wiped the old one from his mind. Gone were the dynamite, the bank, the stacks of twenties, and in their place were sackfuls of diamond, rubies, and pearls. It was true, Chipper admitted, that the new scheme had a concreteness the old one had lacked. Whereas the bank to be dynamited had remained somewhat shadowy in every-body's mind, Miss Sibley's house existed as a hard fact. Furthermore, it had real windows and doors through which boys could crawl late at night. It was just the job for the gang, Pinch concluded, and if Patcher wouldn't let them in on it, they'd do it themselves.

"See," he told the others as they sat in a cellar on a rainy afternoon, occasionally heaving bricks at the rats that came poking around drawn by the buns the gang was eating. "There won't be nothin' to it. Chipper finds out where the stuff is at and leaves a winder or something unlocked. We're in and out of there with bags full of gold and jewels in five minutes."

"Pinch," Chipper said, "who says I'm ever getting into that place? Have some sense." It was becoming increasingly clear to Chipper that Pinch was now his enemy. He had never wanted to be Pinch's enemy, had done nothing to provoke Pinch's ill will that he could remember; but apparently what Shad had told him was true: Somehow, in however confused a way, Pinch recognized that Chipper was his rival to come. Chipper could see, further, that Pinch would try to turn the gang against him. Then were would he be? You were in a lot of trouble if your gang was against you. He would have to be very careful. For one thing, he ought to get out of this business with Patcher as quick as he could. The gang was suspicious of him about it, and Pinch was bound to use that against him. "Look," he said, swinging his eyes around the gang, "I don't have any idea what Patcher's doing with that lady, but he isn't going to share anything with me."

"Chipper, yez knows better," Pinch said. "Patcher's settin' it up. It'd serve him right if we cleaned the place out before he did, after what he done to me."

"Pinch, if you expect me to get anything out of Patcher," Chipper said, "we better not double-cross him right off." This sensible idea seemed to meet with the gang's approval.

Chipper had a chance to talk to Annie and Shad about it later that afternoon, when the rain stopped and the sky began to clear. The three of them went off to the West Side docks at Christopher Street, where the ferry crossed the Hudson from New Jersey, hoping to find suitcases sitting on the ferry dock, waiting to be loaded. But there weren't any, so they sat on a wharf with their legs dangling toward the river five feet below, watching the sun go down over New Jersey and feeling the last warmth of it on their faces. "I wish Pinch would just lay off me for a while." Chipper said. "I'm sick of it."

Shad gave Chipper a look. "I told yez what that was all about, Chipper," he said.

Annie looked from one of her friends to the other. "What? What did you tell Chipper?"

"I said Pinch had it in for him."

But that, Chipper knew, was not quite the whole truth: Shad was avoiding the subject with Annie. "Shad says Pinch thinks I'm trying to take over the gang. I'm not. I never had any idea of that."

There was silence, and they all stared at the great swipes of red and yellow coloring the blue of the sky across the river.

Finally Annie said, "Pinch is okay."

"That's because he's sweet on yez, Annie," Shad said. "He don't get on yez the way he gets on Chipper."

"That's not true," she insisted. "He ain't sweet on me. The only thing is, he's worried Chipper ain't gonna get us into that grand house." She looked at Chipper. "Yez gotta be loyal to the gang, Chipper."

"I am loyal to the gang. Why does everybody keep saying that? The trouble is, Pinch always has these dumb plans that won't work. Who says I'm ever going to see the inside of that house?" Suddenly he wished he hadn't said it, for they were both looking at him.

"What's so dumb about it?" Annie said. "Yez figures out where the jewels and stuff is, unlocks a winder, and we goes in there through the winder and cleans the place out."

Suddenly Chipper realized that so far as Shad and Annie were concerned, calling Pinch's plans "dumb" had been a sign of disloyalty, a clear indication that he was, in fact, trying to start a revolution against Pinch's authority. He could not afford to turn Shad and Annie, his two best friends, away from him. If he had them against him, along with Pinch and Jabber, he'd be finished in the gang. "No, I didn't mean that part of the plan was dumb. I can spy the place out all right, but who says I'm ever going to get inside there? That's all I mean." He looked at them openly so they could see he was telling the truth, but he wasn't: It was a dumb plan.

A day or so later, Patcher made a point of catching Chipper alone when the gang had been wandering through the Fulton Street fish market in its perennial search for food—they had overworked the Washington market. He told Chipper to meet him at the Princess Café at ten that night, which Chipper duly did. Fortunately, Pinch and Jabber had gone off on some venture of their own, which freed Chipper from having to make explanations. They sat at a table near the warmth of the coal fire in the grate.

Behind them the piano was banging, two or three couples were dancing, people were laughing, playing cards. It was even merrier than it had been in there before, because it was earlier in the evening. Chipper and Patcher each had before them a hot punch, and they were awaiting their steak and eggs. It seemed to Chipper that life could be pretty nice at moments like this. Would the time ever come when he could sit in the Princess every night, drinking punch, eating steak and eggs, playing cards, dancing? He hoped it would.

Nonetheless, the wisest thing was to get out of this Patcher business as soon as he could. Here was Pinch wanting one thing, Patcher wanting another, and Chipper increasingly finding himself in the middle. He resented the whole thing. He hadn't asked for any of it. Why was he getting pulled into something nobody would tell him anything about?

"Well, Chipper,' Patcher said, "what cha think of that there place?"

"I couldn't see inside. She was standing in the way."

"Well, I can tell yez, yez won't never see no place richer than that. Why, one of their carpets is worth more than a man can earn in a year."

"She isn't likely to ask me in," he said. Still, he was curious. "What's that round tower for?"

"That?" Patcher said, looking irritated by the distraction, as Chipper hoped he would. "Mostly for show, I reckon."

"Is there a round room inside?"

"Oh yes," Patcher said. "There's bound to be a round

room inside there. Filled with fancy chairs and stuff. Bound to be. Of course, I ain't never been up there meself, so's I'm speculatin', in a manner of speakin', but that's what I reckon." He took a sip of his punch. "What if yez was to see for yerself?"

"I wish I could. I've never been in a round room before."

Patcher leaned back a little and stared at Chipper. "Suppose I said yez might be able to pay a call on that there house."

Chipper blinked and stared back at Patcher. He had not understood him correctly. "I thought you said I could visit there."

Patcher paused for effect. "I did."

Chipper could not imagine himself visiting that grand house any more than he could imagine himself King of England. "I don't get what you're talking about. They wouldn't let me go in there."

Patcher continued to stare at Chipper. "They might. If yez was to play yer cards right."

Suddenly Chipper realized that a good deal more was up than he had imagined. He knew he ought to back off, to get out of the thing, but he was curious. Was there any harm in at least finding out about it? Yes, he reluctantly concluded, there was. "They wouldn't let me in there," he said firmly.

Patcher put his hands behind his head and leaned back in his chair. "Now Chipper, I can see the whole idea of it has taken yez sudden, knocked yez off 'n yer pins, to put it that way. I ain't a bit surprised that it taken the wind out of yez. But yez gotta listen to old Patcher. Yez got to take yer chances when yez sees 'em. Got to be bold about these here things, because they don't come around often. Can't let nothing like this slide by because yez didn't have the courage for it. Got to grab the nettle, in a manner of speaking."

Chipper felt alarmed; all the same, he was even more curious. His role in Dick Patcher's scheme was not to be a minor one, involving, as it now did, paying visits to the rich. The rich were fearsome. What would he say to them? How would he act? Back off, Chipper, he told himself. Just back off. What he said out loud, however, was "What am I supposed to do if I went there?"

"Now Chipper, yez needn't be scared of rich folks. They put their pants on one leg at a time like everybody else, so to say. 'Cept in this case it ain't pants but a dress. Yez just act natural, like yez allus did."

Chipper didn't want to do it. He was scared of the rich, he resented being maneuvered without being told anything, and he was going to be pressured by Pinch to rob the place. Yet he felt himself drawn forward in excitement. What would it be like to go into some rich house where they had . . . what? "What's the idea of it?"

"Aha, there yez are, Chipper. That's just the kind of boy I figured yez was right along. Ready for anything. I figured that right off when I seen yez tumbling out of that there building site. I said to meself right then, that's the boy for yez. That's why I grabbed yer collar so quick. I seen yez was just the boy for me."

A whole array of thoughts were flying through

Chipper's head, most of them going so fast it was hard put to catch hold of them. He said cautiously, "What do I have to do?"

Patcher nodded. Then he looked around the room to make sure nobody was listening. "There ain't nothin' to it. Dick Patcher done all the work for yez. Everything's set. Here's the idear of it. Wednesday afternoon I take yez along to meet that there lady you brung them flowers to."

"At that house?" Perhaps he could ask her to let him see the round room.

"No. Not yet. This here thing's got to go slow. Got to grow like a flower, so to speak. Yez'll go to this here lawyer's office. They'll ask yez questions. A whole lot of them, I reckon. Grill yez good. All yez got to do is tell the truth. Don't lie about nothin'."

Chipper blinked. It was startling to be advised to tell the truth, especially by Dick Patcher. "Just tell the truth?"

"Right. Just the way things was. About yer ma reading yez books, and goin' to her reward, and old Bert O'Connell pounding the tar outen yez whenever he got the chance. And yez runnin' off to join Pinch Mulligan's gang and all that. Just the truth of it."

Chipper was suspicious. Nobody'd ever before proposed that there was any value in telling the truth—except his ma, who'd wanted him to be honest, truthful, and so forth, which admonition he had of course ignored as necessary. "Tell the truth?" he said again.

Patcher nodded. "Except this one little thing. Yez never knowed yer Pa's name, right?"

"No, Ma would never tell anybody." Was he really going to do this?

"That's changed. Now she told yez. His name was Charles Sibley."

"Charles Sibley?"

"Remember that. Don't never forget it. Stick it in yer head so it don't come unglued, in a manner of speaking. Charles Sibley."

"Charles Sibley," Chipper said in a soft voice. He liked the sound of it. In fact, he suddenly realized, he liked the idea of knowing who his pa was, even if he wasn't "Charles Sibley." Still, he knew he should back off.

"That's it. Don't forget it." He looked around the room again. "There's one other thing," he said, keeping his voice low. "All the time yez was growing up yer ma had this ring what wunst belonged to yer pa. Ring with a big green stone set in it. And cut into that there green stone was some kind of funny sign. A sign what reminded yez of a cockaroach."

Chipper nodded. The idea that he might have a father was growing in him. Maybe this Charles Sibley really was his pa. Of course the odds were against it. Still, somebody had to be his pa. He would have to think about it. He said none of this to Dick Patcher, however. "A ring with a big green stone in it that reminded me of a cockroach. Why'd it remind me of a cockroach?"

"It just did, that's all. Reminded yez of a cockaroach. Yez seen cockaroaches in yer time I reckon."

"Lots of them." He nodded and, as an aid to memory, closed his eyes. "A ring with a big green stone in it that reminded me of a cockroach." The ring was beginning to seem quite clear to him mind's eye. "What happened to it?"

Patcher shrugged. "Yez don't know. After yer ma passed on, yez never seen it no more."

Chipper paused. "That's all? That's all I have to remember?"

"That's it, Chipper. Just them two things. Yer ma never told yez nothing about yer pa but his name was Charles Sibley, and she had this here ring of his what reminded yez of a cockaroach."

"How'd she get it from him? Did he give it to her, or what?"

"Yez don't know how she got it. Yez think yez can glue all that in yer head so it don't come unstuck?"

Suddenly Chipper understood that he really was going to meet this lady and tell her this story about the ring and all, and he grew scared. She was rich and could do things to him—have him jailed or whipped or something, if she wanted. Rich people could do such things. "Dick, what if they find out I'm lying?"

"How can they find out? Don't yez worry none, yez'll be fine."

Was it too late to get out of it? He could try. "Dick, I still don't see why I should do it. I don't see what I'm getting out of it."

They were silent for a moment, staring at each other. Patcher was thinking. Finally he said, "Chipper, I ain't gonna tell yez no more about it. But if this thing works out yez could be sittin' pretty. Sittin' pretty. In a manner of speakin'."

It was too late. "I hope they don't catch me lying."

"They won't." Patcher reached across the table. "Shake, partner."

Chipper had no choice but to shake. He was in it now, for better or worse.

Patcher looked around the room. "Well. Here come them steak and eggs. About time, too." He looked back at Chipper. "I'll expect yez at the corner of Broadway and Fourth Street Wensdy at two. I means to take yez to the bathhouse before we meet with this here Miss Sibley and the lawyer. And this time don't bring no Pinch."

Chipper blushed. "How'd you know? I didn't tell them to come, they followed me."

"Chipper, keep it in mind that it ain't easy to put nothin' over on Dick Patcher."

The waiter laid the steak and eggs in front of them. Patcher gave him a look. "Where was yez? Discoverin' the Nile?"

"Yez think yer the only customer I got in here, Patcher?"

Chipper picked up his knife and fork. There was a great deal swirling around in his mind, ideas dancing by in a rush, but the steak and eggs took precedence, and he started to saw away with his knife. There was one question he had to ask. "Dick, was this Charles Sibley really my pa?"

Patcher had a comfortably sized piece of steak speared on his knife and was about to ram it into his mouth. His hand paused in mid-flight. He looked at Chipper rather kindly. "Yez don't want to dwell on nothin' like that, Chipper. It won't do yez no good. This here Sibley fella, he turned up floatin' in the East River a long time ago."

Seven

Elizabeth Sibley sat in the large office of William Hodge, attorney at law. The office was on Pine Street, in the Wall Street area of Lower Manhattan, and had a splendid view of New York harbor. When she turned her head, Miss Sibley could see steam freighters slowly cutting through the harbor, ferries sturdily plowing across from Staten Island, dozens of small craft bustling hither and yon with a certain self-important manner, like terriers carrying home the family newspaper. There was a large Turkish carpet on the floor, paintings of dogs and ships on the wall, the sofa on which Elizabeth Sibley sat.

William Hodge was a man of about forty. "Elizabeth," he said, "I think you must proceed with the utmost caution." They were only second cousins, but had played together a great deal as children in New York nurseries under the eyes of nannies, on the beach in Newport, Rhode Island, where the family owned several "cottages"—in fact rather large, rambling shingled houses fronting on the beach. "Is the boy coming by himself? I think we should talk to him alone."

"The man will get him as far as the lobby. The boy will come up by himself."

William paused to spin the letter opener on his desk. "How did you come across the boy?"

"The man who does odd jobs for me told me about him. He was struck by the resemblance," she said.

"How did he know what Charles looked like?"

Elizabeth did not intend to tell her cousin the truth of that. "He'd seen Charles in his disreputable haunts. It was well known that there was a boy."

William tipped his head slightly. "It was well known that Charles *told* people he had a child. All we have is his word for it."

"Why would he lie about a thing that would bring him into bad odor with the family?"

William put his hand behind his head and leaned back in his chair. "He may have thought that the family would have to buy the woman off. He may have had some scheme to get some money out of it himself."

Elizabeth Sibley stiffened. "Charles would never have done such a thing, schemed as you suggest. You knew Charles better than that. His pride would never have let him. That was one of his problems, his pride." She paused.

"You were too soft with him, Elizabeth."

She said nothing, but turned her head to look out into the harbor.

"And now you want to do something for the boy, is that it?"

Elizabeth tightly clutched the purse in her lap. "William, if he is the boy, we have an obligation to him." But of course that wasn't it. She wanted once again to have the laughing face around her.

William looked thoughtful. "It would depend. First we

would have to determine where the boy came from. That might not be easy.'

"The resemblance is striking. I confess it shocked me." Elizabeth wished she had a higher opinion of her cousin William. As a child she had easily led him around by the nose, which was not what you wanted in a lawyer. But he knew the family secrets.

William leaned forward in his chair. "Has it occurred to you, Elizabeth, that you may be inviting a gang of thieves and murderers into your home?"

"I'm well aware of the risk. I intend to be cautious. But I can't ignore the resemblance. I want you to see him. Today we'll just talk to him."

William looked at Elizabeth, considering. Part of the trouble was that she had never married. There had been a romance twenty years earlier, with somebody not quite suitable. A writer, William recalled. In that respect Elizabeth was rather like Charles, playing by her own rules. Fortunately, the young man had died. She could have married other men: She was good looking and had a lot of money. But she liked her independence. It seemed to William that the death of her parents, the brief romance, and the ugly death of Charles had hurt Elizabeth somehow, more than she was aware. There were rumors that after Charles's death Elizabeth had asked the family doctor for pills or tonic to ease her grief. The doctor had sensibly refused, but apparently she had found another source. You couldn't keep a thing like that from the servants. "Do you really want to bring somebody who's like Charles back into the family?"

She gave the purse a shake. "I would. With all his faults. After Mama and Papa died, he became mine. He was only eight, then, you remember, and I was eighteen. He was all I had left."

William once again took to spinning the letter knife. There were all kinds of dangers. Elizabeth controlled a great deal of wealth. The house on Fifth Avenue and the cottage in Newport were the least of it. More important, there were investments in ships, a copper mine in Montana, a partnership in a railroad in Indiana, a cattle ranch in Wyoming. William was not quite sure how things stood at the moment. Elizabeth involved herself closely in managing her finances, could be quite shrewd in her investments, and did not necessarily consult him. But in other matters she could be extremely foolish. What if she took this boy in and began giving him a hand in managing things? A clever young man doted upon by a foolish old woman could destroy a fortune very quickly. Steal it, spend it, throw it away. William would not personally be particularly affected, but there were others in the family who would, especially their cousin Frederick Sibley. You never knew how things would fall out. Illness, death, childless marriages changed things in unpredictable ways. William's own children might eventually benefit. You never knew. The main point was that rich families who did foolish things often ended up with their fortunes gone. William had seen that happen often enough, too.

Elizabeth, he noticed, was staring at the spinning letter opener. He stopped spinning it. "You forgave Charles a great deal. You took him back again and again when"—

William had been about to say, "he didn't deserve it," but instead said—"others might not have. You were very charitable."

Elizabeth was once again staring at New York harbor. "I knew the good in him. I knew what a wonderful boy he had been. Mischievous, I grant, but there was never anything bad or mean-spirited in him. He was funny. Even as a little boy he made me laugh. A woman will always forgive a man who can make her laugh."

William was well aware that Charles could be witty, for he had often been on the receiving end of Charles's shafts, even though he had been substantially older. Charles had never been respectful of his elders, or anyone else, for that matter. Perhaps it was because his parents had died when he was so young—his mother when he had been two, his father when Charles was eight. Charles could be quite biting. "It's all very well to be amusing, Elizabeth, but can you imagine what he would have done with the money if he had got it?"

"He wasn't to get it until he was twenty-five," she said. She left it unspoken that Charles' body had been fished out of the East River not long before his twenty-fifth birthday. So the money had come to Elizabeth, for her lifetime at least, and would thence go to other cousins, especially Cousin Frederick. William knew that they would be enraged should Elizabeth choose to do something for this street urchin who unfortunately looked like Charles. There would be very expensive and disruptive lawsuits. Family secrets would come out. William decided that he must have a careful look at the terms of the trust. "Elizabeth, I hope you won't do anything without letting me know first." Elizabeth stopped staring into the harbor and turned back to William. "I am a long way from doing anything, William."

At that moment there was a knock on the door. "Yes?" William said.

The door opened part way and a young man put his head through. There was a peculiar look on his face. "Your . . . visitor is here, Mr. Hodge." Elizabeth Sibley felt her heart beat quicken.

Chipper was exceedingly nervous. Too many novelties had come plunging in on him at once. For one, Patcher had taken him to a bathhouse, where he had stripped down and washed himself in a long sink, along with a good many other males of various ages, with a bar of strong, rough, yellow soap. He'd never been in a bathhouse before and, as he had gotten dressed, felt startlingly clean. The kids in the gang swam in the rivers in the summer, and sometimes scrubbed themselves up a little with cold water in church charity sinks, but Chipper supposed he had not been this clean since he'd run off to join the Midnight Rats. While he had been washing, Patcher had beaten the dirt out of his knee pants by slamming them against the bath-house wall, and then he had given Chipper a fairly new blue sweater.

"Not that I wants yez to look like no rich man's boy, but that there sweater of yers smelled so strong it could of walked by itself, in a manner of speaking." A sweater without holes, at least in the elbows, had been a novelty, too.

Then they had taken the trolley down to Pine Street, which had also been a new thing. Chipper had traveled on trolleys before, but that had always been clinging to the rear railing as a nonpaying guest. This time he had had his fare paid and had sat on a bench, feeling rather glamorous. Then Patcher had taken him into the lobby of the building on Pine Street, and had shoved him into an elevator with orders to get out on the eighth floor and find the Hodge & Son offices. The elevator ride had been not merely novel but scary: What if the thing fell? But it hadn't, and Chipper had then found himself in the outer office of Hodge & Son—all brass, mahogany, carpet, pictures—being stared at in some astonishment by a young man in a sharply pressed suit. Then he had sat on a chair, being glanced at from time to time by the young man in the suit, feeling quite self-conscious, with all sorts of questions whirling around in his mind. What was all this about the ring with the green stone? How had Patcher known about it? How had he known about this Charles Sibley in the first place?

More than anything through, Chipper was worrying about being in the halls of the rich. Chipper had always hated the rich. Everybody he had ever known had hated the rich. That was a given. It had been in the air around him, something everybody took for granted. The rich ground down on the poor. They lived high on the hog, enjoying themselves and taking orders from nobody, while the poor worked sixty hours a week, ate potatoes fried in lard for dinner six nights a week, and died early from hard work and slum diseases.

But even so, the rich had to be feared. They were all-powerful, could do pretty nearly anything they wanted to you: cut your pay, take away your job, kick you out of your home, put you in jail. Now Chipper was to go among these people whom he feared and hated. To be sure, there was supposed to be something in it for him, although what, he did not know. Still, he must be wary, wary. But it was too late now to worry about things. He was in it, for better or worse, and he would have to play the game the way Dick Patcher had laid it out. Suddenly he realized that the young man in the suit was beckoning to him, and in a moment he was being propelled into the inner office.

The door closed behind him. He looked around in some bewilderment; here were more brass, more mahogany, more carpeting, and what appeared to Chipper to be a painting of New York harbor until he noticed that the boats in the picture were moving. Where should he rest his eyes? He turned them quickly to the man behind the desk and then to the woman on the sofa, whom he recognized as the lady he had delivered the flowers to. Finally he settled his gaze on the carpet with its strange, wandering design.

"Don't be scared, Chipper," Miss Sibley said. "We won't bite."

How did she know his name? Patcher had told her, he supposed. "Yes, Ma'am."

"I see what you mean about the resemblance," William

Hodge said in a low voice, as if Chipper did not understand English.

"Look at me," the lady on the sofa said.

"Yes, Ma'am," he said, feeling even more nervous. If they caught him lying and got angry with him, they could do anything they wanted to him. They could throw him out the window. Why did she stare at him so? Why couldn't she look somewhere else? And who was he supposed to resemble?

"Come here, Chipper." She patted the sofa cushion next to her. He wondered if he were allowed to walk on the carpet with the strange designs in it, and quickly saw that he could not get to the sofa without so doing. He crossed and sat as far from her as he could get without making it seem obvious. She reached into her purse and drew forth a small package. "Chocolate," she said, "Do you like chocolate? I imagine all boys do."

"Yes, Ma'am." He now understood something that he should have realized before: they wanted something from him, just as Pinch did, just as Patcher did. He should have thought of that, should have asked Patcher about it, although Patcher undoubtedly would not have told him what it was. What could they possibly want from a street boy? Still, chocolate was chocolate, and not to be sneezed at. He took the small package, eagerly unwrapped it, and rammed the square of chocolate into his mouth, leaving a smear on his lower lip, which he soon licked clean. He was about to drop the paper on the floor when it occurred to him that he shouldn't. He looked around for some place to deposit it.

"Here, I'll take it," the lady said. She squeezed the paper into a ball and dropped it into her purse.

Chipper was becoming aware that both of the grownups were watching him intently, and he flushed. It seemed to him that just by sitting there he was doing something wrong.

"His manners want some attending to," the man said.

"Be reasonable, William. He's been living on the streets for five years." She turned to Chipper. "Now, Chipper, I'm going to ask you a few questions. Don't be afraid. if you tell me the truth there'll be nothing to worry about."

The implication was that if he didn't tell the truth there *would* be something to worry about. Nervously he wiped his lips with the back of his hand and then examined the hand to see if any chocolate had escaped him. It hadn't.

"Wants a handkerchief, too."

Suddenly it occurred to Chipper that whatever he might be doing wrong, none of it was his fault. He hadn't asked to come there, hadn't wanted to come there for that matter, hadn't wanted a scrubbing or a fairly new sweater. So what if they didn't like him. He didn't like them, either. The thought gave him courage. "How did you know my name was Chipper?"

"Mr. Patcher told us," she said. "Mr. Patcher told us some things about you. He said that your mother died when you were quite young."

The rich hated people like his mother, who worked in factories. Everybody knew that, because of the way the bosses treated the workers. He was not going to let them say anything about his ma. "Everybody loved my ma. They said she was a saint."

"How did she die, Chipper?"

Why did they want to know about her? What difference did she make to them? "She got something wrong with her lungs from the factory she worked in. She got so she couldn't breathe right and had trouble getting up the stairs. We lived on the top floor. I had to do the errands for her. The shopping and all. Then she got so bad she could hardly get out of bed and I had to do the cooking and such. There wasn't much cooking because she wouldn't eat much. Just wasn't hungry. I tried to get her to eat to keep up her strength, but she'd say she wasn't hungry, I should eat it for her."

"How old were you then, Chipper?"

"Six, I reckon.'

Miss Sibley exchanged a look with her cousin, and then back to Chipper. "How old are you now?"

"I'll be thirteen soon."

"She died in eighteen eighty-eight, then?"

"I guess so," Chipper said. "It must have been around then." He was feeling a little less scared. The lady—Miss Sibley was her name, he remembered—looked dangerous, but she spoke in a kindly fashion. Perhaps she wasn't as dangerous as she looked.

"What was she like? Was she pretty?"

It had never occurred to Chipper to wonder whether or not his ma had been pretty. He tried to recall her face. "Sure," he said, hazarding a guess. "Sure she was pretty."

"And intelligent, would you say?"

This, too, was a question that had never occurred to Chipper. He considered. "She read a lot of books. She was always reading me books. About King Arthur and legends of the Greeks and such. She was always on me about my speech. She said respectable people didn't say 'ain't'."

Miss Sibley's eyebrows went up. "She liked to read? I'm surprised. Most people of her class—" She stopped. "A great many people are not much interested in books."

"Oh, she was always reading. When she got sick she had me go to the library all the time for books. It was the only thing she could do."

"Where do you suppose she learned to like books?"

It was beginning to be clear to Chipper that there was something important about books. He wished now that he'd read more since he'd joined the gang. But they'd have teased him about it. "From her pa. He was in the printing trades over on Hudson Street. He made her talk right, the way she did me."

"Printing trades?"

"He was a book binder. He used to bring home books from the bindery, Ma said." Then without thinking: 'Stole them, I reckon." He remembered where he was and flushed. Why on earth hadn't he had more sense than to say that?

Miss Sibley glanced at William. "That would explain some things," she said in that low voice that they assumed Chipper could not understand. She turned back to him and smiled. "I can think of worse things than stealing books."

That was a surprise. He had expected at the very least to get a lecture on the evils of thievery. Instead, she seemed to think it was all right, in the case of books at least. The rich, it appeared, were not exactly what he had thought them to be. "He used to read to Ma just the way she read to me. Then he died when she was twelve or something, and the younger ones didn't get read to as much. Aunt Millie and those. Ma said it was a shame, because she had got some education out of it and Aunt Millie hadn't."

"Did you love her, Chipper?"

What kind of a question was that? "My ma? Everybody loved her. At the service Father Murphy said Ma hadn't an enemy in the world and would surely find a place in Heaven."

"But did *you* love her?"

The question was confusing. Chipper wasn't quite sure what it was to love somebody, but he supposed that it was the same as liking somebody, only more. "I guess so," he said. "If she ever got some extra money she'd buy me something with it." Chipper had not had a chance to talk about his ma for some time. But this lady—he must try to think of her as Miss Sibley—wanted him to talk about her, and he was glad. Miss Sibley seemed to think his ma was okay, even if Pinch didn't.

"What else?" she asked.

"Oh, I don't know. She was just nice, is all. Everybody said so." Suddenly Chipper became aware of slight motions from the direction of the desk. He turned his eyes. The man sitting there had a pen in his hand and was writing.

Now Miss Sibley touched his shoulder. "And what about your father, Chipper?" she said softly.

They wanted to know about him, too. Well, so did Chipper. But he didn't know anything about him, and here was where the lies began. He started to get nervous again. He had been telling lies as a matter of routine since he had been turned over to the graces of the O'Connells, to the point where at times he hardly knew when he was lying and when he wasn't. But lying to Uncle Bert or Pinch, who assumed he would lie, was quite a different matter from lying to these rich people. They began to seem dangerous to him again, wild animals waiting to pounce should he make the smallest misstep.

Suddenly he realized he had forgotten the lies he was supposed to tell. That was even worse, because Patcher would be enraged with him if he didn't get his lies straight. He felt himself flush again. Desperately he tried to calm himself so he wouldn't begin to drip telltale sweat. "I don't know much about him," he said, stalling. "Ma wouldn't talk about him. I always asked her, but she wouldn't tell me." Then, vastly to his relief, it began to trickle back into his mind. "All she ever told me was his name."

"And that name . . . ?"

He couldn't remember. He flailed in his head helplessly. Then it came. "Charles Sibley. She said his name was Charles Sibley."

The man at the desk stopped writing and leaned forward. "Are you sure of that, Chipper? You didn't seem sure."

"I'm sure. You're making me nervous with all these

questions." Talking back to them made him feel a little more confident. "His name was Charles Sibley." Now he remembered about the ring.

Miss Sibley nodded. "What would you expect, William? Be reasonable. It's a very strange circumstance for Chipper."

It almost seemed as if she might be on his side, Chipper thought. The man wasn't: He hated Chipper the way most rich people did. But perhaps she didn't hate him so much. At least it seemed like that. Still, he must be wary, wary. He said nothing about the ring, but waited.

The man stopped writing but went on holding the pen. "When were you born, Chipper?" he asked.

Patcher had told him to tell the truth, as much as possible. It was less dangerous, anyway. "June thirteenth."

He wrote. "What year was it?"

Chipper was aware that both were watching him closely. Something about his birthday was important. His instinct was to lie, but Patcher had said to tell the truth. "Eighteen eighty-two."

The adults exchanged a look, and the man wrote something. Then Miss Sibley said, "Chipper, during the time your mother was sick and couldn't work, who was paying for your food and rent?"

He shrugged. "I don't remember." He was beginning to get the hang of telling the truth. He found it surprisingly comfortable. "I don't guess we paid the rent. Aunt Millie and Uncle Bert must have paid for our food, I reckon."

"Aunt Millie was your mother's sister."

"Yes. They lived three blocks away, over on Crosby, between Broome and Spring." He wondered if he ought to be telling them all this, but he needed to work around to the ring. "Ma got on with Aunt Millie pretty good. Not so good with Uncle Bert, though. When she got real sick she made them promise to take care of me. Aunt Millie promised, but Uncle Bert, he didn't like me. He was always swatting me, so finally I ran off."

The man behind the desk went on taking notes. "I'm curious about your gang."

Chipper was again wary. Rich people, he assumed, would not like kid gangs, because they stole and did other nasty things. Could they put him in jail if they knew he stole? He felt danger around him. "You have to be in a gang if you live on the street. It's too lonely and scary if you aren't."

"I'll bet your gang is pretty tough," the man said. "Fighting, stealing, and so forth."

Chipper saw the trap. "We don't steal if we don't have to. You don't want to take the risk." How could he get off this subject and lead the conversation around to the ring? Patcher would kill him if he didn't get that in.

The man sat with the pen poised over the piece of paper. "What kind of things did you steal, Chipper?"

What sort of lamebrain did he think Chipper was? "We don't steal much. Too risky. We beg, mostly. Sell newspapers. The girls sell flowers."

The man made a note with the pen. Then he said, "Chipper, your aunt and uncle. They're still alive?"

"I guess so." He hadn't seen them for some time, but he assumed word would have drifted his way had either of them died.

"Their last name is?"

"O'Connell."

"And their address?"

As much as he hated Uncle Bert, he wasn't going to give them away to this rich man. "I forget," he said. "I haven't been there in a while."

The man looked at Miss Sibley and said in that low voice Chipper was not supposed to understand, "We can find it. They'll be in the city directory."

There was a brief silence, and then Miss Sibley said, "Can you remember anything else about your father, Chipper? Anything at all? Your mother must have talked about him to you."

Suddenly having a father was giving Chipper a rather curious feeling. Odd, but nice. He reminded himself that he didn't really have a pa, he ought to be sensible about it: But try as he might, the feeling kept growing in him that this Charles Sibley—whoever he was—might be his pa after all. Besides, it was a way to bring up the subject of the ring. "She didn't want to talk about him. She said we had to forget about him, it didn't do any good to dwell on it." He stopped, and then, trying to be as casual about it as he could, he said, "She had a ring that used to belong to him. At least she said it had."

Both of the adults held still and stared at him intently. "A ring?" Miss Sibley said. "Did you ever see it?"

"Oh yes. It had a big green stone with a design carved into it."

The adults looked at each other in silence. "Now, Elizabeth . . ." the man said.

She turned back to Chipper. "What sort of design, Chipper?"

Once again Chipper tried to appear casual. He shrugged. "I don't know exactly what you call it. A funny design. It looked like a cockroach, sort of. Well, I don't guess anyone would put a cockroach on a ring."

There was more silence. "Elizabeth," the man said once again.

But Miss Sibley did not hear him. She had leaned forward to stare deep into Chipper's face. Her hands were clenched over her purse so tightly that her fingers were blotched with red and white spots. "Are you sure, Chipper?" she whispered.

Chipper could sense that he had gotten onto very dangerous ground. This seemed to be the lie that mattered, which meant it was very dangerous and might lead him into trouble. They might even kill him. The rich didn't mind killing poor people, Chipper knew, for they worked them to death all the time. But he couldn't change his story now; Patcher would kill him instead.

So he said, "I'm sure. I saw it a lot."

Miss Sibley went on staring at him intently. "And the ring had a bug of some sort incised into it. A beetle, perhaps."

It would be more convincing if he were a little uncertain. "It could have been a beetle. I don't exactly know the difference. All I remember is that when I was little I was scared it would get off the ring and come after me." That was a good touch, Chipper knew.

There was more silence. Then the man said in his invisible voice, "Elizabeth, there could be a dozen explanations."

She looked at the man and relaxed a little. "I'm not a fool, William. I'll need to know more." She turned back to Chipper. "Where's the ring now, Chipper? Do you know?"

Patcher had told him that he didn't know where it was. "I don't know where it went. After Ma died I never saw it again. Maybe she was buried with it." That was another good touch.

She looked at the man, who nodded and made a note. Then she turned back to Chipper. "I'd like you to come visit me at my house, Chipper, so we can talk some more. Will you do that?"

He wasn't at all sure that he wanted to. He was curious, yes; it would be interesting to visit there. It was also true that this woman appeared to be friendly, bringing him chocolate and taking his side on some things against the man. Nonetheless, the rich were cruel; they were the enemy. He didn't want to be drawn in against his own people. "I don't know if I should," he said. It wasn't much of an answer, but it was the best one he could think of.

"Suppose I discussed it with Mr. Patcher. Would that help?'

That most emphatically would not help; Patcher would be enraged if he learned that Chipper had turned down an opportunity to visit the grand house on Fifth Avenue. So, Chipper realized, would Pinch. Whether he liked it or not, he would have to go. Too many other people would insist on it. "Okay," he said. "I'll come."

"Wednesday at four, then?" she said. "I think you know where the house is. We'll have tea."

She stood. Now that it was over, he wanted nothing more than to get out of that office with its mahogany, brass, and carpeting and back into the homey comfort of the Midnight Rats. He did not walk, but ran out of the office and, ignoring the elevator, ran down eight flights of stairs to the street below. Only when he had put five blocks between him and Pine Street did he finally slow to a walk.

In the mahogany and brass office Elizabeth Sibley and William Hodge sat in silence until they were sure that Chipper was out of hearing. Then Hodge said, "It's coincidence, Elizabeth. You mustn't let your emotions run away with you. Charles was hardly the only person who owned a scarab ring." William Hodge had learned a long time ago that emotions were dangerous. You had to control them, not let them control you. He recognized that he sometimes appeared cold and unfeeling to others—even to himself, occasionally—and that perhaps he was lacking in some way. Still, he was willing to accept the loss, for it meant living life on a more even keel.

"It sounds exactly like the one grandfather got in Egypt when he was there helping to finance the railroads."

Hodge shrugged. "Still, many people had them."

"The birthday works out,"she said. "He was born two months before Charles died."

Hodge shrugged again. "How many boys were born in New York City around that time? Thousands, I expect."

"What about the boy's face?"

She was getting stubborn, Hodge realized. She had been stubborn as a child, always insisting that the cousins do things the way she wanted. As a child William had been bossed around by her often enough. But that was over now. "Elizabeth, you must have more proof. I insist. All you have is the facial resemblance and the story about the ring. You don't have the ring itself, mind you."

"Obviously these O'Connell people sold it when the mother died."

"Perhaps," he said. "On the other hand, the whole thing might have been a fabrication. You said that this man Patcher had seen Charles often enough to have noticed the resemblance to Chipper some years later. He could have remembered the ring, too, and coached Chipper in the story."

Elizabeth flushed slightly. She had lied about Patcher knowing Charles. Unlike Chipper she was not used to lying. "Charles was not wearing the ring when he was found."

Hodge noticed the faint flush on his cousin Elizabeth's cheeks. She was lying about something. He had to talk her out of this. Apparently she didn't realize the uproar it was going to cause in the family. There would be endless expensive lawsuits, hard feelings, valuable financial partnerships jeopardized. Poor Frederick would be livid with rage. "Elizabeth, you must have more proof. There are others in the family who are concerned."

She sniffed. "I'll decide for myself, William. As for others in the family, they can look out for themselves. They're not my responsibility. I shall do as I choose about the boy."

Eight

"What was it like?" Annie asked. It had begun to rain again, and they were holed up in a cellar on Sixth Street, amid the damp smells, cobwebs, and the scuttling sounds of rats.

I was never in such a place," Chipper said. Now that the adventure was over, he was feeling a little proud of himself for having had an experience that the others were unlikely ever to have, and he wanted to boast a little. "They had so much new stuff in there it was like a furniture store. Eight stories high. There was a big window and you could look down on the tops of the ships. You could see the whole harbor."

Pinch, however, was concerned less with the romance of the situation than with more practical matters. "What did they want out of you?"

Suddenly Chipper felt the air go out of him, and he didn't feel like boasting any more. It was beginning to seem as if everybody were now his enemy. They all wanted something from him, and there was no possibility that he could satisfy one without angering the others. How was he going to answer Pinch? The gang simply took it for granted that Chipper would use the situation to their advantage, whatever that might be. It would not cross their minds that he might have to take into account the needs of Dick Patcher and even the desires of the rich people. It was just hopeless. No matter what he did, somebody was going to be angry at him. He was stuck. "She wants me to go over to her house and have tea." Chipper knew that was not really what Pinch wanted to know.

"Patcher's tryin' to get yez in the house to scout it out."

"I don't know what Patcher's scheme is, Pinch. He didn't tell me. All I know is, I'm supposed to have tea with her." Now he wished he had done what he had known he ought to have done and got out of Patcher's scheme when he had had the chance. But it was too late for that.

"Just tea?" Annie said. 'Won't she give yez no sandwiches and cake or something?"

"I don't know,' Chipper said. The same thought had occurred to him: Tea, to Chipper, was a chipped mug with milk and sugar such as his ma and Aunt Millie used to have when they got together. "She didn't say."

Annie's eyes were shining. "I bet she gives yez cake and pie and sandwiches and cookies and stuff. I wisht I was goin' with yez."

"I wish you were, too," Chipper said. He would feel a whole lot more comfortable going up to that grand house with a friend from the gang.

"Forget about them sandwiches, will yez, Annie," Pinch said. "Think about what's in that house besides sandwiches. Diamonds and pearls, gold rings and bracelets laying all over the place. Heaps of silver. Yez can buy all the sandwiches yez wants once we get ahold of the stuff." His eyes were sparkling, and he danced lightly from one foot to the next. "When Chipper's up there he'll slip a ring or bracelet in his pocket just to show yez."

But Patcher had warned him about precisely this. He had said, "When yez go up there for tea, Chipper, it'll come into yer head to slip somethin' in yer pocket—spoon, little silver dish. Wouldn't be natural if yez didn't. Anybody would think of it." He had paused, put his hands on Chipper's shoulders, and had given him a little shake. "Yez mustn't touch a thing, Chipper. Yez mustn't take a second spoonful of sugar unless they offer. We got much bigger fish to fry in this here thing, in a manner of speakin'." He had shaken Chipper again. "Yez hear me, Chipper?"

Patcher had been making himself abundantly clear, and Chipper had averred that he had, in fact, heard. Patcher had shaken him once more, to make sure that the idea was stuck well in place. "Not so much as a spoonful of sugar, Chipper. Yez mustn't throw away a big chanst over no spoon."

Chipper did not like being shaken, and he was getting very tired of everybody's telling him what to do. What big chance was Patcher talking about? A big chance for Patcher, clearly, or he wouldn't have been going to all this trouble; but how come nobody would tell Chipper what was in it for him or why the rich people were interested in him at all? Something to do with this Charles Sibley and his fancy ring, no doubt, but what? Maybe the ring was worth a lot of money and they wanted to find it. That seemed as close an answer as Chipper could find. Well, it wasn't going to do them any good to have him to tea—he didn't know where the ring was.

And there was Pinch, demanding that he steal something from the house, and Patcher certain to smack him around if he did. Suddenly Chipper was fed up with the whole thing. Maybe he just wouldn't go when the time came.

Dick Patcher clearly had considered that possibility and, two hours ahead of time, he turned up and beckoned to Chipper with his forefinger. "Time for yer bath, Chipper." The gang laughed and Chipper blushed.

"Yez'll laugh outta the other side of yer mouths when yez see Chipper risin' up in the world without yez."

Chipper gave Pinch a quick glance. Pinch took out of his jacket pocket a folding knife, opened it, and began grooming his fingernails with the blade. He spit into the street. "Chipper knows who his friends is," he said.

Patcher ignored that. "I don't want none of yez follering after Chipper, neither. Yez hear that, Pinch?"

Pinch looked at Dick Patcher with his head aslant. "I heard yez runnin' yer mouth, if that's what yez means." He appeared to be as relaxed and casual as if he were out for a Sunday stroll, but a muscle was flickering in his cheek. Still staring at Patcher, he stopped grooming his nails and ran the ball of his thumb over the knife edge.

"Pinch, if I dint have better things to do, I'd of taken that toy away from yez and shoved it down yer throat. But I ain't got time for it now." He looked around at the Midnight Rats. "If I catches any of yez follering after Chipper,

I'm gonna fix yez so yer own ma wouldn't reckonize yez, if yez ever had such a thing." He jerked his head. "Come on, Chipper, yez and me had got better things to do than gas with this bunch."

Chipper knew he couldn't leave it like that: He had to say something to the gang. "I'll be back before night," he said. "I'll tell you about it." Then he trotted after Patcher.

They had hardly got around the first corner, heading toward Fifth Avenue, when Patcher stopped and looked at Chipper. "Now, Chipper, yez listen to Dick Patcher. Yez got a big chanst in this here thing. Yez can't listen to what Pinch tells yez no more. Yez gotta stick with Dick Patcher. The sooner yez break away from them Midnight Rats, the better, to put it that way." Then he turned and led Chipper toward the bathhouse.

As soon as Dick Patcher, standing across the street from the grand house on Fifth Avenue with the round turret, saw Chipper disappear behind the closing door, he turned and proceeded with quick strides in a southeasterly direction toward a certain two-room apartment on Crosby Street. Shortly he was sitting on the sofa, trying to settle himself among the loose springs. "I knew yez would want to have word of the boy," he said.

Bert O'Connell was seated in the easy chair as if it were part of him. From time to time he carried to his mouth a beer mug. "Oh," he said, "Millie was troubled," as if being concerned about others was not worthy of a man.

Millie O'Connell nodded. "It bothered me some, I have to tell yez, Mr. Patcher. I wasn't sure we done the right thing. Me mind wouldn't rest easy."

"Oh, yez was bound to feel that way. Wouldn't of been human if yez didn't. A woman would. It shows the love yez had in yer heart for the boy."

"It was me poor sister Emmy what troubled me. I'm sure meself it was best for the boy. But what would she of said? Sometimes I feel her eyes starin' down at me. It makes me shiver."

"Well, let me put yer mind to rest, Mrs. O'Connell. Yez couldn't of done nothin' better for the boy. Couldn't of done nothing better for him if yez was to send him off to Harvard College. I got it fixed so's he's got a chanct to break away from that there gang what's corrupted him, snatchin' purses, robbin' drunks, who knows what all. Got him a job apprenticin' in a livery stable, nice warm hayloft for him to sleep in, all meals pervided, and fifty cents a week besides. Now ain't that a step up for the boy?"

Millie O'Connell's eyes brightened. "Will wonders never cease. I wouldn't of thought nobody would of took on a boy like that."

"They wouldn't of. Not with the gang he's runnin' with. But I begged and pleaded, I come near to gettin' down on me knees. I promised if there was the first sign of trouble I'd make good on it meself. So the fella said he'd think about it, and yestidy he come to me and said, 'Patcher, I woun't do it for nobody else, not knowin' what I do about this here boy, but you allus been straight as a die with me and I'm gonna give the boy a chanct.' It was deliverance for sure. But of course this here fella what owned the livery stable, he wanted to be sure there ain't any question about it. I showed him this here paper what we signed the other day. He said that was fine so far as the boy's ma goes, but what about the pa? And I said to meself, 'What about the pa?' So I figured I best come around so as to clear the matter up."

"Fifty cents?" Bert O'Connell said. "He's to get fifty cents a week? That don't seem right to me, not after all the money we spent on him year after year, feeding him and clothing him and treats. By rights he oughtta turn the money over to me."

"Oh, I'm sure of it," Patcher said. "No doubt of it. And maybe he will, once we get this here thing settled. Even better, I could pay up a few weeks in advance." He glanced at Bert. "Once we get the thing settled."

"From what you said it was settled," Bert O' Connell said, setting the beer mug on the floor the better to concentrate his mind. "I thought yez said it was settled."

"And it is settled." Patcher paused. "Just this one little thing. The pa." He paused again and looked from Millie to Bert and back again. "I got to put his name down on this here paper." He touched his jacket to indicate which paper he had in mind.

Bert O'Connell started at Dick Patcher. "What're yez gotta do that for? We already signed."

"Yes, I know," Patcher said, holding onto his temper. "And that's well and good. But we gotta get the pa's name down. We gotta know who he might be in case somewheres along the line somebody was to go after that fifty cents. I couldn't pay no advance on the boy's wages if there wasn't going to be no wages, so to put it." He paused. "Now somewheres along the line yer poor dear sister, God rest her soul, must of let the fella's name slip out. Stands to reason she would. Wouldn't of been natural if she didn't. Would of said, 'Bill Jones told me the other day,' or 'Henry Smith wouldn't hurt a fly,' or 'Frank Green give me a bonnet for me birthday.' Some such. Bound to have slipped out like that somewheres along the line."

Millie frowned and shook her head. "She was mighty close-mouthed about him. Wouldn't—"

"Now hold on there a minute, Millie," Bert said. "Now that I think of it, something like that did slip out." He looked at his wife in a meaningful way. "Maybe yez wasn't there when it slipped out. But some name like that slipped out. I remember clear as day." He paused and looked at Patcher. "How much of advance was yez thinking of?"

"Say ten weeks. About as much as I could afford, seeing as it's comin' out of me own pocket. Times is hard."

"Make it twenty. Ten dollars."

"Split the difference. Seven-fifty."

Bert frowned. "It seems little enough after what I spent on the boy."

"What seems little comin' in, seems a lot goin' out, so to put it." He reached into his jacket pocket, pulled forth some coins, and counted out the money. "Now what was this here name the pore dear woman mentioned? Was it Bill Jones? Henry Smith?"

"That was it," Bert O'Connell said. "Henry Smith. That was the boy's pa. That's what she said. This here Henry

Smith was goin' to buy her a bonnet but had forgot. 'That Henry Smith,' she said. 'He plain forgot about me bonnet he promised.' He was the boy's pa. I'd swear it on a stack of Bibles." He scooped the coins out of Patcher's hand.

If Bert O'Connell would swear to the boy's parentage on a stack of Bibles for seven dollars and fifty cents, what, Patcher wondered, would he swear to for ten dollars? However, he did not ask. Instead he drew from his inside pocket a piece of paper which he had had carefully drawn up by a full-fledged lawyer a day or so earlier. The O'Connells signed, and now Dick Patcher knew that he had bound Chipper Carey—or whatever his last name might turn out to be—to him indissolubly for the lifetime of them both.

As Chipper stepped into the front hall, and the maid in the white apron closed the door behind him, he was stunned by the wealth around him. From pictures in magazines the gang had occasionally found in garbage heaps, Chipper had been made aware that the rich, by which he meant anybody who had a house of their own, lived in a style that was entirely foreign to him. He had expected to see handsome, comfortable chairs, large, shiny tables, pictures hanging on the walls. But as he gazed into the rooms visible from the hall, he saw an opulence he was entirely unprepared for: so many chairs and sofas he could hardly count them, clad in shining fabrics of a multitude of colors; not just a pair or two of candlesticks but forests of them, some of glass, some of silver, some of other kinds of metal he could not identify; not just shelves of books but whole walls of them;

not just a carpet on the floor but fields of them, in soft rainbows of colors; and hanging from above, rainfalls of crystal candelabra descending from the ceiling like the glittering drops of a sun shower. And everywhere there was light, bouncing from silver candy dishes, from brass drawer pulls, from gold clock finials, from the crystal showers descending from the ceilings. It was, finally, the light that unnerved him, for it seemed that the rich had not only more light than the poor but light of a richer, more glowing quality. He stood in the hall, holding his dirt-stained cap in his hand, sure that the rich must think and feel different sorts of things from what he, Pinch, Patcher, Aunt Millie, his own ma did. He could not imagine that anyone who lived among such light-drenched surroundings could ever feel pain, terror, longing, the sense that the world was against you. That could not be possible in this place.

There was plenty to steal, in any case. The solution to his dilemma, he had decided, was find something small to steal that wouldn't be missed. That way Pinch would be satisfied, and Patcher would never know. He had wondered whether there would be such a thing in the house; but now that he stood there waiting for Miss Sibley he could see plenty of small stealables: small silver candy dishes, silver candle snuffers, letter openers, and more. He was making a judgment about what might most easily be taken without being missed, when Miss Sibley came along the hall toward him. Hastily he took his mind off the subject of stealing, in case she could somehow see into his head, which at this point would not have surprised him.

"We'll have tea in the sitting room, Chipper. There's something I want to show you in the parlor, but we'll do that another time." She gestured to the maid, who disappeared.

The sitting room appeared to be much the same as everything else, filled with furniture, curlicued and polished and flooded with light. "Why don't you sit in that chair, Chipper, and I'll sit here where I can look at you." She sat on a yellow sofa with a pattern woven into it. Chipper looked at the chair she had indicated, which matched the sofa. Chipper knew that his knee pants were none too clean. "I don't know as I ought to sit there," he said. "I could sit on the rug."

"Don't be silly, Chipper. Sit in the chair."

"I might get it dirty."

"It can be cleaned."

Suddenly Chipper understood another thing: Not only did the rich—Miss Sibley, anyway—have a great wealth of things, they had behind them so much money that it didn't matter if something got dirty, damaged, broken; they would simply get a new one. So he sat on the chair.

In a moment the maid returned carrying a small folding table, which she set down between Miss Sibley and Chipper. Behind her a second maid was carrying a tray, which she placed on the folding table. Chipper saw that Annie had been right: There was on the tray a china teapot entwined with red roses and green leaves, a matching sugar bowl, a matching creamer, a matching slop bowl, matching teacups and saucers and any number of spoons, forks, and knives.

There was also a plate on which reposed a large amount of chocolate cake; another plate with apple tarts; a bowl of chocolates; and a small dish of some sort of candy Chipper could not identify. The smell rising from the tea tray into Chipper's nose almost raised him from his seat. He closed his eyes and licked his lips.

"Cake or tart, Chipper?"

His eyes switched hungrily from one to the other.

Miss Sibley smiled. "Perhaps you would like some of each, to see which you like best."

"Yes, Ma'am."

She dug into the food with the cake slicer and handed Chipper a plate. "I think you might call me Miss Sibley, Chipper. Ma'am is what the servants use. Friends call me Miss Sibley, and I hope we're going to be friends."

Chipper knew he ought not to be sucked in by all this food and nice talk. The rich were the enemy, and he should be cautious, wary, find out what she was after. In truth, however, it was hard not to be sucked in. When was the last time anyone had fed him tea and tarts and spoken nicely to him? It was hard to resist. "Yes M— Miss Sibley," he said. He was beginning to realize that the rich had their own way of doing things, and he decided that it would be worth his time to learn them.

She poured each of them a cup of tea, with cream and sugar, and sitting straight on the sofa, said, "I want to know a great deal about you, Chipper. Fair exchange for the tea, I think. Tell me first about your mother."

Patcher had told him that as a general thing he was to

tell the truth. Not that he trusted Patcher, nor intended to follow his instructions as if they were the word of God; where he was only suspicious of Miss Sibley, he had no doubts that Patcher would sink him if there were five cents in it. Thus, as he couldn't think of anything wrong with telling the truth, he decided to do so simply because that way he wouldn't be caught lying. "She was born on the West Side. That's where my grampa lived before he died. Grampa came from Dublin. He was apprenticed to a printer there, and when he was a boy he used to meet these famous writers when they came into the printer's shop. Ma said he knew a lot of them. She told me their names, but I forgot them."

"He had some education, then."

Chipper was not sure what constituted an education. "I guess so. He read Ma books when she was little, the way she read to me. They had a nice apartment when she was growing up, Ma said. Men in the printing trades did real well then, Ma said. They had nice furniture and such. He wanted Ma to get an education and become a school teacher. That was the great thing, Grampa said. They were starting a lot of new schools then and Grampa said there would be a big call for teachers."

"That is true. With so many new people coming in who couldn't read and write or even speak English, it was felt that a great system of public schools was needed. But she never became a teacher?"

"No. Grampa died and there wasn't any money anymore and she had to go to work to help support the little ones.

So she never finished her schooling. She was bound I would. She said I was to get my schooling and rise up. But Uncle Bert, he wouldn't hear of it. They said they didn't intend to work their fingers to the bone while I sat around living off the fat of the land."

"I'm glad to know about your mother, Chipper," Miss Sibley said. "She must have cared for you a great deal."

Chipper's eyes shone. "She always said I was her pride and joy. She said she'd been her pa's pride and joy, and I was hers."

Miss Sibley looked out the window into the branches of the trees that grew by the house. Chipper was sure she was thinking about him. It felt strange to have this rich lady thinking about him. But Chipper also had a practical turn of mind, and he took the opportunity to wet his thumb and pick up from the plate the remaining crumbs of cake and tart. Miss Sibley turned back and smiled. "Perhaps I could persuade you to have another slice of cake. Or perhaps, now that you've tried them both, you would prefer a tart?"

Among his own kind the general idea was to stuff yourself at every opportunity on the grounds that you never knew when you'd get anything more. Chipper sensed that it was probably different with the rich, and that the politest thing would be to say no, thanks. The second politest thing, obviously, would be to choose either tart or cake. But he couldn't help himself. "Could I have both?" He had, however, the grace to blush deep red. "I couldn't figure out which I like best."

"Chipper, you can have as much cake and tart as you like."

What was going on? Why was she being so nice to him? He didn't even have to be polite. "Thank you, Ma'am— Miss Sibley."

"Tell me about your gang."

The Midnight Rats, Chipper realized, was not a subject he could talk about quite so openly as he had talked about his ma. "It's just a regular gang," he said, at the time stuffing a good chunk of tart into his mouth just in case he said something wrong and she changed her mind.

"And what do you do to earn your keep?"

What could he tell her? That they rolled drunks, snatched purses, scavenged the refuse heaps in markets for food, took anything from anywhere that wasn't nailed down? Was he to tell her that they fought other gangs for the right to corners where begging for pennies was likely to be good, that they fought among themselves over nothing? "Oh, different things," he said. "The boys mostly sell newspapers. Shine shoes. The girls are mostly flower girls." All of this was true, but you'd starve to death pretty quick if you depended on shining shoes or selling flowers. He decided to change the subject back to his ma. "Ma would hate to know I got into a gang, but I couldn't stand being whacked by Uncle Bert all the time."

She would not be switched, however. "It is my understanding that gangs such as yours live mainly by stealing." She raised her teacup and watched him over the rim. Her eyes, he noticed, were gray like his, and did not waver. He began to feel uneasily that she might not be easy to get around. "Oh, we wouldn't think of stealing, Ma'am.

We have a rule against it in the gang."

"Miss Sibley, please, Chipper."

"Miss Sibley."

She put the teacup down. "Now, Chipper, I am not a fool."

He blushed. She *was* going to be hard to get around. "Maybe, sometimes, some of the kids, might, maybe take something they shouldn't ought to. If they were real hungry."

She went on looking at him. "Frequently you steal."

He looked down at his plate. "Frequently we steal."

"In fact, stealing is your primary occupation."

He went on looking at his plate. Why wasn't she being nice to him anymore" "Stealing is our primary occupation," he whispered into the plate.

"And you have been wondering ever since you entered this house what you could slip into your pocket."

He sat bolt upright and stared at her. Momentarily their gray eyes met. He looked down. Could she actually see into his head? He flushed hot and began to sweat. "No, no, I—"

She held up her hand. "Chipper, if we're going to be friends, we have to be honest with each other."

He sat there stunned and uncomprehending. He had not realized that they were going to be friends. He had not been able to figure out what she wanted from him, but it had not occurred to him that it was simply to be friends. The idea that friends had to be honest with each other was also a new one. He was friends with Annie, Shad, Jabber, and some of the others; had been friends with his ma, certainly; was sort of a friend with Dick Patcher as well. It had never crossed his mind that he ought to be honest with them just because they were his friends. You lied to your friends when it was necessary. He paused. "I—I . . . Yes, Ma'am."

"Chipper, I don't blame you for thinking of stealing. I have so much and you have so little. But you don't have to steal from me. If you need something, I'll give it to you."

He raised his head to look at her, feeling confused and unsettled. The rich were turning out to be much stranger than he had thought, in ways he still didn't understand. What did she mean, she would give him what he needed? He stared at her, not sure that she meant it. "What would you give me, if I asked for it?"

She went on looking at him. "What do you need?"

He needed everything. He needed a different life. "Would you give me some cake for the Midnight Rats?"

"Of course. I'll have them put up a box of things for you to take with you. Cake, tarts, candy . . . I suppose they'd like candy, wouldn't they?"

She meant it. He sat there stunned. In his entire life, nobody had ever offered him whatever he needed. Nobody had ever offered him *anything* he needed, aside from secondhand trousers and potatoes fried in lard. He could see now that pocketing something from this grand house had been a very bad idea right from the beginning. Pinch had been wrong about that and Patcher had been right: There was too much to lose. In his bewilderment, Chipper was not able quite to grasp what there might be to lose, but it wasn't just a question of money—or even mainly a question of money, no matter what Dick Patcher thought. At least for Chipper it wasn't. He couldn't quite put a name to what might be in it for him, but it wasn't money.

In any case, he no longer wanted to steal anything from Miss Sibley's house. He was changed, somehow. How and why he was not sure, either, but his world, with a sudden jolt, had shifted, and he was now a blind man, feeling his way with his hands in a strange place. Anyways, it was clear that Pinch was wrong about the whole thing. Somehow he would have to get the gang to see that. "Miss Sibley, how did you know we steal? Did Dick Patcher tell you?"

"No. Chipper, you must understand that in New York the gangs have grown enormously in recent years. They were not nearly so big nor so dangerous when I was a child. I suppose it's because of recent hard times, poverty, all the new immigrants. You should realize that the newspapers are full of stories about the gangs. All of this is well known."

"The Midnight Rats were in the newspaper?" He wished he'd seen the story.

"I can't say that your particular gang has been written about. But similar gangs, yes. The children's gangs are no secret."

"Oh," he said, feeling disappointed. If they were going to write about a gang, they should have chosen the Midnight Rats, for surely it was the wickedest and most daring of the kid gangs.

"Perhaps some other time they'll write about the

Midnight Rats," she said. Then she rose and offered him her hand. "Chipper, will you come back and see me next week?"

He saw that the tea was over, and stood, too. He realized, somewhat to his surprise, that he was sorry to be going. He would have liked to stay there some more. The whole time he had been there, his mind had been so full of so many things, like whether he was supposed to hate the rich, and being sucked in, that he had been unaware of another feeling. This was how exciting it was to be in the places of the rich, to be awash with money. Why it was exciting, he was not sure. It was, he decided, probably the way you would feel if you got chosen leader of your gang. "I'd like to come again,' he said. So they arranged the time.

For a moment Miss Sibley stood in the doorway, watching him go. A variety of emotions chased each other through her, coming and going. It had been exhausting. She turned, and went up the broad stairs to her room. She really must, sometime soon, try to break herself of this habit of taking a draught of her elixir when she felt tired and unnerved. She wished she hadn't got into the habit in the first place. She should have had more fortitude, more willpower. But the death of Charles had been one blow too many. And then it had gotten to be a habit.

Well, she would stop. Very soon. But not just yet, not at this moment when so many conflicting emotions were chasing through her. She mixed the draught in her Venetian glass with the harlequins running around it and lay down on her sofa under a light blanket, and soon she was in a hazy dream of a laughing boy splashing up flurries of pigeons in Washington Square. Only, this time the boy was a little different.

Nine

"A box of cake?" Pinch said. "Some candy? Is that all, a box of cake?" They were sitting in a rough circle on an East River pier as the sun eased down behind the city, making the river dance and sparkle. The air was rich with the smell of hot tar and dead fish. "That house's loaded with diamonds, silver, jewels."

Chipper was determined to hold his ground. He knew he was right about not heisting anything out of Miss Sibley's house. He was no longer quite so sure that he had anything to gain by treating Miss Sibley right—being honest, not stealing—much less what "anything" was. The feeling he had had in Miss Sibley's living room, that it wasn't about money but something else, was fading under the harsh light of the world he lived in. It was funny: In Miss Sibley's house, he didn't want to steal from her; now that he was back with the gang, he felt different about it. She had so much and they had so little. Somehow, she'd made him forget that the rich were the enemy.

Yet despite all this, he knew he had been right not to pocket anything. Pinch was wrong. For the good of the gang, never mind about Chipper, they ought to see that Pinch's plans weren't any good. "Look, Pinch, she knew I was planning to heist something. She said so."

Pinch's brow wrinkled in disbelief. "What? She told yez that? Wha'd she ask yez there for if she knew yez was gonna heist something?"

Chipper saw that he had said the wrong thing, for if he tried to explain why she had told him she knew he intended to steal something, it would lead him back into the idea that she would give him whatever he needed, and that would make them extremely suspicious. "Well, she didn't exactly say that. She said she knew about our gang stealing, it was all in the papers. She had her eye on me the whole time."

"We was in the papers?" Annie said. "I never knew that."

"Not exactly us. Kid gangs."

"How come they didn't put us in?" Pinch said.

"Come on, Pinch, that wasn't Miss Sibley's fault."

"Miss Sibley is it, now."

Chipper looked around. He knew he had to appear unafraid. "Well, what of it? You all want me to get friendly with her, don't you?" He paused and looked back at Pinch. "Pinch, even if I was to see a way to heist something, I oughtn't do it." He remembered how Patcher had put it. "There's much bigger fish to fry. We don't want to throw it away for a couple of spoons."

"Like what?" Pinch demanded. "What fish?'

Chipper realized that the truth was his best argument. That was rather startling in a world where in most instances the truth was nothing but trouble. "I don't know," he said. "You gotta give me time. But if I get caught heisting a candlestick or a silver candy dish, she'll throw me out and that's all we'll ever get out of the place." He looked around at them. They said nothing, but there were slight noddings of the head here and there. Chipper was astonished by the efficacy of the truth. He decided to push his advantage. "So you see, Pinch, I was right not to pocket anything. We oughtn't to heist anything yet."

"Pinch, Chipper's right," Shad said.

Pinch put his hands on his hips and thrust his jaw forward. "Chipper's gettin' too big for his pants, in my opinion." He was confused and angry. "You better decide who yer with, Chipper—us or that there old lady."

Chipper saw that he had won, that he had shown the Midnight Rats that he had been smarter than Pinch in this case. But he also saw that Pinch, whatever his mental capacities, had hit upon the crucial point: Whom indeed was he with, the gang, or Miss Sibley? Chipper was far from sure. It troubled him. He had gone into that grand house with a clear sense that the rich were the enemy and fair game for anything he could get out of them; he had come out of that house an hour later not at all sure who the enemy was, except that, alarmingly, one of them appeared to be Pinch. How had that happened? Had she put some kind of a spell on him? Next time he would resist the spell and cling to the gang, which had, after all, been his only support and sustenance for years. It was troubling; and he decided, as he usually did when he was troubled, to consult his amulet, the golden sovereign hidden behind that brick.

So he wended his way down Mulberry Street through the early evening throng going home from the sweatshops, the pushcarts, the butcher shops, and bakeries, their faces dirty, their bodies weary; thence down the narrow alley smelling wetly of sewers, and into the musty, cobwebbed, dimly lit, forgotten storage room. He pulled the brick from its niche, took out the coin, and stood by the door in the shadows so what little light there was could fall on it. "Well, all right," he said softly. "Which is it? The gang or Miss Sibley?" Could it be both? He supposed that he could probably persuade Miss Sibley to give him money for the gang from time to time; or what was more likely, clothes, baskets of food, perhaps even a room for them to sleep in during bad weather. His experience with charity ladies was that they never gave you money, for fear you would spend it on beer or card games; it was always something you couldn't spend, like shoes or sweaters although he'd seen boys gamble away their shoes often enough on *stuss* games.

No matter what she gave them, though, they would still want to rob her. That Chipper knew. They had grown up in worlds without futures, worlds where you took whatever you could get *now*, because prior experience had taught them to expect from the future more of the same.

This, it occurred to Chipper, was perhaps where he was different. His ma had been forever talking to him about his future—how he was to get his education and learn to behave like respectable people and rise up in the world. His ma had believed that it was possible to rise up, because she had come down. Her pa had not been a day laborer, a pick-and-shovel man, but had been one of the "princes of labor," as they were called, a man with a skill and a trade, who could earn double or triple the wages of a day laborer.

They had had a four-room apartment, a piano, books, a pretty table lamp with a stained-glass shade which had shone red, green, and blue light on his ma's nightshirt as she had sat on her pa's lap being read to until she had fallen asleep.

Chipper had had at least the idea, if not the actuality, that you could rise. The other kids he knew, especially the ones in the gang, had not had that. Pinch had lived six people in two rooms and had got hit one way or another every day. Annie had been left to take care of three younger children at the age of eight, spending her days, not in school, but desperately fighting the little ones to keep them from falling out of windows or setting the apartment on fire. They had no reason to think you could rise.

So if they saw an opportunity to steal, they would. Chipper knew as well as he knew the shape of his hands that soon enough they would want to pillage Miss Sibley's house. He could not prevent that; he could only stall. So the question remained: the gang or Miss Sibley? It could not be both. It was unfair. All she wanted from him was to be friends. Have tea, maybe do some other things together, like . . . what? Go for a ride in her carriage or something. Maybe she would buy him new shoes when he needed them—she'd said she'd give him whatever he needed. Did he dare to ask for shoes? They were expensive. Why couldn't he be friends with her? It wasn't hurting anybody.

But he saw that he couldn't. He needed the Midnight Rats. Miss Sibley might be good for cake, tarts, a pair of shoes, a new cap. She might even be good for whatever it was that wasn't about money. But the Midnight Rats were good for everything else—people to sleep all tumbled up with on cold nights, people to steal with, to cook beef stew with, people to fight with, laugh with, cry with. He could get along without Miss Sibley; he could not get along without the gang.

He went on looking at the sovereign for a long time, feeling sad about the way things in life were, tracing with a dirty fingernail the scrolly C cut into it, and occasionally turning it over to see if something might turn up on the other side. Nothing did, so he sighed, rubbed up the coin a little to assure it that he would not neglect it, and put it back in its hiding place.

William Hodges was sitting behind his desk in his office with the splendid view of New York harbor, awaiting the arrival of his cousin, Frederick Sibley, who was second cousin to William and first cousin to Elizabeth. William was not pleased with his cousin Elizabeth, which was why he had suggested that Frederick drop in at the office. The Hodges and Sibleys had all grown up together, first and second cousins indiscriminately, in large New York City houses, in beach houses in Newport, occasionally in the Tuileries Gardens in Paris or Hyde Park in London. Later they had gone to the same boarding schools in New England, the same colleges, also in New England, the same balls and parties in New York, Boston, and Newport. They had courted each others' schoolmates, and sometimes married them.

There was a good deal of money scattered through the

closely related Hodge and Sibley families. It was, however, scattered unevenly. Some of them had a lot of it; some of them relatively little—that is, they might not have more than two or three servants, only one coach, and only a share in a beach house. The key point was that money follows blood. It thus mattered a great deal who was related to whom, and exactly how closely. With the disposition of millions of dollars depending upon it, rich families always knew fine degrees of relationship. Everybody was well aware that Frederick Sibley, due to the death of the unfortunate Charles, was now closest in degree of relationship to Elizabeth. Everybody was also well aware that Frederick, who was almost forty and not yet married, had only a brownstone house, two servants to look after him, and a three weeks' share in a Newport cottage.

As matters now stood, Frederick was first in line to inherit the trust from Elizabeth. If Charles and Elizabeth's parents had lived to see Charles grow up and go bad the way he had, they might have made other arrangements. But they hadn't lived. So the estate had been left in trust for Charles, under the control of Elizabeth until Charles reached twenty-five. Charles had never reached twenty-five. When his body had been pulled from the East River by a juvenile wharf rat, the pockets full of water and nothing else, it had come out that the dead man had run up large gambling debts and had been known to drink heavily. A verdict of suicide had been brought in.

William, however, was fairly confident that Charles had not killed himself. That was not Charles's way—he enjoyed his life too much. Probably he had been drunk and fell off a boat. Perhaps he had been robbed and murdered. Still, it was best to let people believe it was suicide. Why raise a lot of questions?

Frederick Sibley was announced. He was tall, like many of the Sibleys, and slim, with a rather long head, the length emphasized by a hairline that had receded almost to the crown of his head. Frederick sat casually on the sofa with the view of the harbor, his long legs stretched out. For a moment the cousins bantered, discussing another cousin's race horses that had had a habit of finishing dead last, and then Frederick said, "But you didn't ask me here to talk about Cousin Edgar's horses."

"No." William leaned back in his chair with his hands behind his head. With Elizabeth he always felt that he had to be slightly deferential. Feeling that way irritated him, but it was a habit he had developed in childhood and could not shake. However, William had a great deal more money than Frederick, and it was up to Frederick to defer to William. "Have you heard about this slum boy that Elizabeth's taken up?'

"I heard some far-fetched story, but I didn't put any credence in it. Elizabeth's always taking in strays. It never lasts."

"This one might."

Frederick became alert, his pale blue eyes blinking rapidly, his long forehead wrinkling in alarm. "Are you serious, William?"

"Yes. She thinks the boy might be Charles's child."

"Oh, my God," Frederick said. He sat for a moment

stunned, as the implications rose up around him, like water around a man trapped in a tank. "But there can't be anything in it. Why haven't we heard of this child before?"

William was rather enjoying his cousin Frederick's anguish and was in no hurry to end it. "We did. Not long before he died, Charles told Elizabeth there was a child. A boy. He came to me about it. He wanted to settle something on the mother. Naturally I stalled. I didn't want any formal acknowledgement of the boy's existence, on which he might base a claim later. Let Charles give her some cash if he felt he had to and let it go at that."

Frederick was white. "Why this woman? He had so many, beginning from the time he was fifteen."

William, still sitting comfortably with his hands behind his head, shrugged. "As hard as you may find this to believe, Frederick, Charles may have been in love with her. Both Charles and Elizabeth are people of strong feelings, and they act on them. That is probably regrettable, but in an odd way I always respected Charles for it. Foolish, of course, but I respected him for it."

"How can you respect it, William? In the end he had to take his own life."

William said nothing, but turned his head to stare into the harbor.

"William, surely you're not implying—"

William took his hands from behind his head and snapped upright. "I'm not implying anything, Frederick. I'm not sure that it would make any difference in any case. It's the boy who's the problem."

"He can't really be Charles's son. It's some delusion of Elizabeth's."

William nodded. "Probably. The odds are certainly against his having anything to do with Charles. But there's some evidence. For one thing, he looks amazingly like Charles. Not a twin, of course, but the resemblance is marked."

"That's not enough to go by."

"Not by itself, no. But Elizabeth brought him up here and we talked to him. At one point he let it slip that his mother had once had a ring that sounded very much like the green scarab ring Charles always wore. The one that belonged to your grandfather."

"I always wanted that ring. What happened to it?"

"Assuming it was the same ring. Let us assume that for the sake of argument. Charles gives the ring to the mother. The mother shows it to the boy, has it around the house. The boy—" He picked up a piece of paper from the desk. "I made a few quick notes when he was talking. He said, 'It had a big green stone with a design carved into it. A funny design. It looked like a cockroach to me. It scared me when I was little. I was afraid it would walk off the ring and get me.'"

"There are hundreds of those scarab rings around. Not ones as valuable as that one, I'll grant, but the boy wouldn't know that."

"There aren't many in Irish slum apartments."

"Unless they were stolen," Frederick said.

"Usually quickly sold."

Frederick was silent for a moment. "All right, where is it, if they ever had it?"

"The boy's mother died when he was six." He looked at the paper again. "In eighty-eight or thereabouts. Her sister and brother-in-law took the boy on. I have no doubt that they sold the ring before the woman's body was cold."

Frederick was looking a little less pale. "So there's no evidence for the ring but the boy's word."

William looked out the window again. "He brought it up without prompting. It didn't come out of anything we said."

"Elizabeth might have coached him beforehand."

"Elizabeth hadn't talked to him previously. She wants to know the truth. Granted she's romantic and hopes that this is in fact the right boy. But she hasn't gone completely mad."

"William, surely you wouldn't testify that the ring was Charles's."

William waited, thinking. Then he said, "As matters now stand, I would have to testify that the boy appeared to know about it without prompting."

"Would *have* to?" Frederick said loudly. "Would *have* to, William? You know my situation. Our side never had very much. Father's bad luck with the cotton mills and so forth. You know all that."

"Frederick, it isn't an outcome I want, either. But I am not going to perjure myself."

Their eyes met. Frederick said, "So you believe the boy might be Charles's son after all?"

William shook his head. "No, I don't. There are too many improbabilities. There's nothing to connect this woman to Charles—no letters, no photographs, nothing of the kind. There's no birth certificate—Elizabeth had that searched years ago. Of course, that means nothing. We can assume that the child was born at home, with a midwife in attendance instead of a doctor, and nobody bothered to register the birth. It happens all the time in the slums. For another, Charles must have met scores, hundreds of women in his low Bowery dives. Why this one, why this boy? There's nothing but the facial resemblance and the boy's memory of the scarab ring. It'll need more for Elizabeth to make a strong case. But still, it won't be easy to prove her wrong in court even without further evidence. Charles was known to have haunted these Bowery places where he might have met this woman, and he told people, including me, that there was a boy. And—" He glanced at Frederick. "—the dates work out. I made a point of asking him for his birth date. He was born two months before Charles died." He hesitated. "I checked my old diary. Charles came to see me about the woman a month after the boy was born."

"The boy could have known when Charles died and concocted a suitable birth date."

"That would suggest that the boy knew things about Charles, wouldn't it? I don't think we want to go in that direction."

Frederick was silent for a moment. "How did Elizabeth come across this child?"

William shrugged. "I'm afraid that Elizabeth is not being entirely candid about that. She appears to know a young man from the Bowery who, as she puts it, does odd jobs for her. I suspect there's more to it, but I can't tell you any more than that." He paused and patted the desk. "No, I don't believe he's the son. But Elizabeth might be able to convince a court of it, assuming she believes it herself. I'd just as soon that didn't happen."

"She can't do anything without a court order?"

"Not if somebody fights it. A court might prevent her from giving the boy anything at all, except pocket change. It might hold that she couldn't use any of the trust money for the boy's support unless there were strong proof that he was Charles's heir." He began sorting through the papers on his desk. "Now Frederick, there's the couple who took care of the boy after the mother's death. He lived with them for several years before he ran off to the gang he runs with now. Their names are—" He looked over the papers. "—Bert and Millie O'Connell. Living at 79 Crosby Street." He paused. "There might be something there."

"Are you suggesting—"

William quickly held up his hand. "I'm not suggesting anything. I merely mention it." He wanted nothing to do with it. If there was dirty work to be done, let Frederick do it. He stood and looked at his watch, "I'm sorry, but I've got another appointment."

Ten

As Chipper walked into the grand house on Fifth Avenue and followed the maid across the wide entry hall toward the sitting room, he was determined that he would not let Miss Sibley suck him in again. Yes, she was being friendly as could be; yes, Pinch had it in for Chipper and might even do him harm.

Even so, the rich were the enemy, and the Midnight Rats were his friends. They were people like himself; they were him, in a way. He knew them all, knew their ways, knew when to trust them and when not to. What, on the other hand, did he know about Miss Sibley? What was she up to? What reason did he have to trust her?

Patcher, Chipper was sure, knew something about what was going on, but he also knew that there was no point in asking him: Patcher would tell him what it suited him to reveal, which might be all lies anyways. Whatever the case, he would not be sucked in again.

Miss Sibley was sitting at the tea table, which was set as before with the rose-entwined tea service, the spoons and forks, except that this time there was gingerbread and a cut glass bowl full of whipped cream to spoon over the gingerbread. Chipper's ma had made whipped cream for him once for his fifth birthday, so he knew how good it was, but he had not had it since. He licked his lips, then realized that licking your lips was probably not polite and put his tongue back inside his mouth.

"Chipper, I'm curious to know more about how you live. We won't discuss stealing, I'm not asking you to incriminate your gang. Just how you live: where you sleep and what you do all day." She poured him a cup of tea, cut him a large piece of gingerbread, and spooned a good deal of whipped cream over it. "Where do you sleep in cold weather, for example?'

Information was the price of the gingerbread and tea. "We have some cellars we get into through windows. Mostly they're in real old buildings where nobody lives anymore but are used for storage." Talking, he realized, was getting in the way of the gingerbread. He sawed off a large chunk with his fork, smeared it around in the whipped cream and jammed it in his mouth. It made him choke and he had to take a swallow of tea to wash it down.

"But how do you stay warm?"

"You make a stove out of an old five-gallon lard can. Punch holes around the sides near the bottom so as to allow for a draft and burn coal if we can find it, or else busted up packing cases. We sleep kind of heaped up. It isn't too bad."

"In good weather you sleep outside?"

"You want to sleep under a bridge in case it rains. The Brooklyn Bridge is good. Put down some cardboard, wrap yourself in newspaper under your shirt. It's all right."

"And you scavenge for food?"

He realized that there might be an advantage in getting her to feel sorry for him—when you went begging you tried to look thin and sad so people would pity you. But somehow he didn't want her to pity him. Why should she think she was better than his gang? "We don't eat too bad," he said. He sliced off another large chunk of gingerbread and swirled it in the whipped cream. "We generally can get hold of some potatoes, onions, carrots, stuff like that. If we have ten cents we can buy a chunk of beef, stew it all up in a lard can over a fire."

She raised her teacup and looked at him over the rim, as was her habit. "Chipper, did you ever wonder if you couldn't have some other sort of life? Instead of sleeping under bridges and scavenging for food?"

His ma had wanted him to have a different life, that was certain. But that was over: He hadn't got his education. "No. How could I?"

"Don't you want to have a different life, Chipper?"

That confused him. As he had not believed he could have a different life, it had not occurred to him to wonder if he wanted one. "I'm kind of used to it. I just go on from day to day like always."

"But you needn't," she said. "There's an entirely different world around that most people live in. A world where people eat proper meals three times a day, sleep in beds every night, wear clean clothes, are polite and kind to each other instead of fighting and cursing as I imagine you do."

He didn't like her saying such things, for it made it seem that the gang wasn't as good as other people.

"We do all right. Down there an awful lot of people don't eat much better than I do. When I was living with Aunt Millie and Uncle Bert we ate mostly bread, beans, potatoes fried in lard, stuff like that. We didn't eat too much gingerbread."

"Yes, I know," she said. "I've read books. I've seen Jacob Riis's pictures of the slums. Working people live hard lives, I know that. But for a well-spoken boy like you with some brains there are ways out of it."

"How?" She was trying to talk him into something. He was determined not to get sucked in. "Leave the gang. Get a job with a future." she paused. "Wasn't that what your mother wanted for you?"

It had been. He was to get his schooling and find some kind of a job where he could rise. Not long before his ma became bedridden, she had begun to bring home books from the library about boys who "Moved Up." It hurt him to think that he was letting her down. Well, she would be proud of him if she could see him now, having tea with this rich lady in this grand house. No question where his ma would have stood on it: Get out of the gang and trust to Miss Sibley. He could almost hear her: "Chipper, it's a wonderful opportunity for you, how many boys get a chance like this," and so forth. He turned his head to look out the window at the backyard, where there was a swing, flower beds, a stone bench. He knew he was getting sucked in again. "It isn't so easy to get a good job."

He thought she would offer some advice about jobs, but she didn't, and he was glad to be out of that conversation.

"Come with me, Chipper. I want to show you something. We'll finish our tea later."

Chipper rose, giving the whipped cream a glance. As she turned her back to lead him away, he ran two fingers around the inside edge of the bowl, scooping up a large dollop of whipped cream, which he sucked into his mouth. He wiped his fingers on his shirt.

She led him across the entryway into a more formal room, which she called the parlor. It was on the north, uptown side of the house and looked out onto the carriage drive, which ran around to the stable behind the house. Across the graveled drive was a line of large forsythia bushes, now blooming bright yellow. The parlor contained a small grand piano; several sofas in red and yellow cloth— silk, he supposed; the usual Oriental carpet; the usual crystal chandelier twinkling in the sunlight. Miss Sibley, however, was looking at a portrait over a sofa near a window. It was a large picture, about three feet wide and four feet high, showing a boy of about ten sitting on the stone bench in the backyard, with a medium-size dog at his feet. Chipper did not know much about dogs and could not identify the breed. The boy was wearing a pair of blue trousers, a shirt ruffled around his neck, and a big floppy pink bowtie.

Miss Sibley pointed. "Look at the boy's face, Chipper."

Being large, the picture was hung fairly high on the wall, so that most of it was well above Chipper's head. Nonetheless, there was plenty of light in the room and he could make out the face without difficulty. A strange excitement, as if he had seen magic, crept into him. Chipper had not seen his own face very often. The O'Connells had a small mirror, but it was so mottled that you could make yourself out only by moving your head around. However, he had looked often enough in shop windows at things he wished he had and had seen his face mirrored in the window glass. There was no doubt about it: He and the boy in the picture looked a lot alike.

For a moment he stood there stock-still, too filled with shivery magic feeling to think—excited and scared. He was now beginning to glimpse, however vaguely, the shape of things behind the mystery.

"Who does he look like, Chipper?"

"Like me," he whispered, his voice shaky. "He looks like me." His heart was pounding, and he felt the magic all around him.

"Go closer, Chipper. Look at the left hand."

He moved closer, standing with his legs against the sofa that sat under the picture, on tiptoes, his head tipped back. The boy's right hand was reaching down to touch the head of the dog. On the left side of his stomach was a watch fob with a round gold decoration of some sort on it. Chipper had heisted watches from drunks often enough to know that the chain or little leather strap you pulled the watch out with was called a fob. The boy's left hand lay on his left leg. There on the index finger was a large ring with a green stone. He kneeled on the sofa to bring his face closer to the ring. Sure enough, incised into the stone was some sort of a bug—a beetle, they had said. The bug that had scared him so much when he had been a little boy. He turned to face Miss Sibley. "Was he Charles Sibley?"

"Yes. He was just eleven when that portrait was made. He was a wonderful boy."

Chipper turned back to the portrait, the queerest feeling coming over him. Was it possible that this boy, just a little younger than he was now, had grown up to become his father? Why not? Somebody had to have been his father. The world, it seemed to Chipper, had become brighter.

And then he remembered that his ma had never said anything to him about Charles Sibley, that he had never heard the name until not long before, when Dick Patcher had told him to glue it into his mind. Nor had he been frightened of the bug on the green stone, for he had never seen the ring until that moment, and that was only in a picture in any case. It was all lies. The world grew dark again.

"What are you thinking, Chipper?"

He didn't want to answer, didn't even want to turn around to face her. It was all lies, and he felt sick of himself. Still, he had to face her, had to choke down the rest of the gingerbread before he could leave.

He stood there, pretending to examine the picture. Why were the lies bothering him so much? He'd told thousands of lies before—to the Midnight Rats, to Patcher, to Aunt Millie and Uncle Bert, to his teachers back when he was going to school, to shopkeepers, even to his ma. Thinking about it, he could see that he'd lied more often about things than he had told the truth. But somehow this time it was different. Why? What was so different about it? Different because he could not for the life of him think of anything she wanted from him, except to feed him tarts and gingerbread and all those things that weren't money. Different because she trusted him. Had anyone else ever trusted him this way? Well, his ma, but that wasn't the same. Anybody else? Not really. Annie sometimes. Maybe Shad sometimes. But in the world he came out of, who would trust anybody? Whom would you trust? Everybody needed everything and scrapped and scrambled to get it. Miss Sibley, however, had everything and could afford to trust. He had betrayed her.

"What are you thinking, Chipper?" she asked again.

Slowly he turned around, knowing that he had to go through with it. "That's the ring," he said, forcing himself to meet her gaze. "I'm pretty sure of it." And then, to make himself feel a little more honorable, he said, "I might be wrong. I haven't seen it for six years, since Ma died. Maybe I could be wrong."

She cocked her head to examine him. "But you believe it's the same ring."

He really had no choice. He took a deep breath. "Yes. I think it is." He had got sucked in again.

Bert O'Connell was both bewildered and uneasy. A few minutes before, there had come a knock on his door. When he had opened it, expecting one of the other tenants in the building to be standing there asking to borrow half a loaf of bread, a quarter, a blanket, he had found instead a gent in a fancy suit, cravat, gold watch fob which he ought to have better sense than to wear around that neighborhood. The man had not given his name, but had said that if Mr. O'Connell would give him a few moments of his time, he would make it worthwhile. Bert O'Connell had, of course, been suspicious, but clearly the gent had money and perhaps could be persuaded to part with some of it.

So he had asked the gent in, and now it was Frederick Sibley's turn to try to find a comfortable place to situate his bottom among the protruding springs of the O'Connell sofa. "Get the gent some tea, Millie," he had ordered, but Frederick had refused the offer. So now the O'Connells were sitting in their accustomed places, Bert in the easy chair which he seemed a part of, Millie in the straight chair at the table.

"I don't believe in beating around the bush, Mr. O'Connell," Fredericks said. "It is my understanding that you are guardian of a boy known as Chipper Carey."

Bert remained perplexed. This was the second person to come around asking about that ungrateful kid. First it was that fella Patcher, and now this gent. He could not fathom what the value was in the boy; but if Patcher had been willing to cough up seventeen dollars and fifty cents, this gent must be good for at least as much. "Well, yes, yez could say we're guardian to him" To be sure, he had signed away rights to the ungrateful kid, but this gent was hardly likely to be on confidential terms with Dick Patcher.

Millie nodded. "His pore ma, she begged us to take him with her last breath. But we couldn't do nothin' with him, no matter what we tried. Bert, he was like a father to him, but finally he run off."

"So I understand," Frederick Sibley said. "Actually, it's the boy's father I'm interested in."

"That's funny," Millie said. "This Mr. Patch—"

"Millie don't know nothin' about it," Bert put in quickly. "This here Patcher wanted to 'prentice the boy to a livery stable if I'd come up with ten dollars, but I wouldn't. I told him the kid wouldn't be able to stand two days' honest labor and would run off, and I'd be out the ten dollars."

Frederick took a breath. "Yes, no doubt. But you knew the father."

Bert poked around in his brain in hopes that something would turn up, but nothing did. What sort of father did this gent want? "Well, maybe we did and maybe dint, as the sayin' is."

Frederick took another breath and looked at Millie. "As the mother's sister, surely you knew the boy's father."

"She was awful close—"

"Millie don't know nothin' about it." Bert was remembering that he had signed some sort of paper at Patcher's behest stating that the father was . . . was who? He couldn't remember. "Yes, we knew him," he said. "But like Millie says, Emmy didn't talk about him too much."

"He gave her a ring, I understand."

"What?" A ring? A ring? Bert didn't remember any ring. Had Millie found it and sold it? That would have been very wrong of her. He gave her a look.

"He might of for all we know," Millie said.

Frederick pounced. "You know nothing of any ring? A ring with a big green stone in it?'

"Now hold up a little, Millie," Bert said. "Let's put our thinking caps on." Did the gent want there to be ring or not be a ring? "This here ring, it was gold, was it?"

"If you'd seen that big green stone you wouldn't have forgotten it," Frederick said.

Bert began to sense that the money was on there not being a ring. "Suppose I said we never seen nothin' like that."

"I don't beat around the bush, Mr. O'Connell. It'd be worth your while."

Bert nodded sagely and looked at Millie. "Yez never seen no such thing, didja, Millie?"

"No, I never did, Bert."

Frederick leaned forward. "And surely if your dear sister had owned such a ring she'd have shown it to you. Flaunted it, no doubt."

"Flotted it?" Millie said.

"Showed it off. Polished it up and worn it about."

"Oh, she'd of done that all right," Millie said. "She thought she was better than ordinary folks. She'd of flotted it all right."

"But you never saw it."

"We never seen her flot it."

Frederick reached into his vest pocket and drew forth a small purse which he jingled. "That's useful information, Mr. O'Connell." He extracted a twenty-dollar gold piece from the purse. "Now, about the father. You say you never met him?"

Once again Bert was unsure of where the money lay. "I dint say we never laid eyes on him." He looked at Frederick's face, trying to find a clue. "Or that we dint."

"But surely you knew his name?" He looked at Millie. "It was your own sister, who lived three blocks away, more or less."

Apparently the gent wanted there to be a father. But Bert had already given Patcher a name. What was it? He poked around in his brain again. "Jones, I think it was. She was mighty close about it. Or Smith." Once again he searched Frederick's face for a clue. "Some such name as that."

A tiny smile crossed Frederick's lips. Jones, Smith, it didn't matter. "But it wasn't Sibley."

"What'd it be worth if it was or wasn't."

"Not much if it was."

Bert nodded. "Jones was what it was. A Bill Jones. Sure as I'm sittin' here."

Frederick now stood. "I appreciate your time." He opened his purse and extracted another twenty-dollar gold piece from it, which he laid on the table. "Now, I may need you to sign an affidavit. Nothing complicated. I can have it drawn up in a day or two. You can sign your name, Mrs. O'Connell?"

"Why I never heard of no such thing," Millie said. "Of course. We had our schooling."

"Good."

But Bert was alarmed. "Now hold up just a sec. I don't know as I want to sign no affidavit."

Frederick smiled. "I know it's a nuisance. I'd be willing to pay for your time. How does a hundred dollars sound?"

A hundred dollars? Bert sat there, stunned. He'd never seen a hundred dollars together in his life. And here it had just walked in through his door.

Eleven

"I don't see what we're waitin' around for," Pinch said. "That place is loaded with diamonds, pearls, rubies, silver, watches, a safe full of money, millions of bucks' worth." He danced from one foot to the other, his eyes shining. "What're we waitin' for? Chipper, yez got to get us in there soon."

They were once again in the musty, cobwebbed cellar, avoiding a gentle spring rain that fell onto the cobblestones and made them shine. It was afternoon, and they were eating bread, cheese, and bologna, which they had purchased with the proceeds from a purse they had snatched from a woman on a trolley earlier in the day. Annie had climbed up onto the side of the trolley with her begging can, and when the woman lifted her purse from her lap to give Annie a coin, she had seen her chance and snatched it. She had flung it down to Jabber and they had fled out of sight, like a school of fish, before the woman could open her mouth to scream.

Chipper had known it was coming. He had now been up to the house on Fifth Avenue four times for tea. He had also gone for a ride in her carriage up Fifth Avenue to Central Park and then back down again. It had given Chipper an astonishing feeling to be riding along behind a coachman, looking out on the pedestrians slightly below him. Miss Sibley had also bought him a new shirt and a new pair of socks. Chipper supposed there would be more of the same. He didn't understand it. It had to do with the picture of the boy on the parlor wall, of course. Who, exactly, was Charles Sibley? Chipper had given this question a good deal of thought. He was not Miss Sibley's son, he didn't think: She didn't seem old enough to have been his mother. Who, then? He wasn't sure.

It was beginning to embarrass him that he had told her and that lawyer that Charles Sibley was his father. He realized now that they couldn't possibly have believed it. It was too far-fetched. How would his ma and Charles Sibley have ever met? True, a lot of swells came down to the Bowery to visit the theaters and saloons there; it was just possible that they could have come across each other somehow in a shop or on the street. Chipper had read stories in the magazines they found about a man and a woman seeing each other across a room and knowing instantly that they were meant for each other. Maybe something like that had happened. But it wasn't very likely.

It didn't make any sense. Miss Sibley had to have some reason for being nice to him—serving him tea and tarts, buying him new socks, taking him for rides in her carriage. Chipper couldn't figure out what it was, but it was something. He wouldn't let himself get sucked in again.

And yet, there were moments when he was at the house with Miss Sibley and they were chatting in a friendly way about things, when he found himself believing that Charles

Sibley was his father after all, and that he belonged there, having tea. He would have to be careful of that.

Now the pressure was on him to get the gang into the house. As much as he didn't want to get sucked in by Miss Sibley, he didn't want to rob her, either. Not after everything she'd done for him. They'd got to be friends, in a way, despite Chipper's resolutions not to get sucked in. How could he think of robbing her?

He could stall, at least. "It isn't going to be as easy as you think, Pinch. They have servants all over the place in there. The least noise and they'll come swarming down on you—us." That was certainly true. One of them would knock over a chair in the dark or sweep a glass bowl from a table and wake the house. They had never attempted a job of this magnitude before; it had always been purse snatchings and pilfering from shops and pushcarts. They had no experience at large-scale robbery.

"Them servants gotta sleep sometime. We'll go in there real late, two, three in the morning when they're dead to the world. They won't hear nothing'."

"You're kidding yourself, Pinch. Somebody's bound to wake up."

"Naw, they won't. Now what you got to do, Chipper, is make a map of where everything is. Where they got the jewels, where they put the silver teapots and stuff at night. Map it out real good so we don't go fumblin' around in there. Then yez gotta unlock a winder somewheres that ain't under no street light. We'll go in there. Each of us told what to go for. We'll be rich. We'll be in for thousands apiece. I tell you thousands. Won't be sleepin' in cellars no more, nor wearin' rags what come out of garbage cans." He rubbed his hands again and jigged from foot to foot.

Chipper looked at the others. Like Pinch, all they could see were jewels, gold, heaps of dollar bills. They couldn't see a servant with a lamp and a pistol, the police pouring in through the doors. Pinch could enthrall them with his talk of gold and jewels, because he believed in it himself.

"Look, for one thing I can't go wandering around the place making a map. I've never even been upstairs."

"Get her to show yez around. She's got all them diamonds and pearls in her bedroom like as not. Get her to show yez in there."

"She probably won't. I can't just get her to show me things." He paused. "Look, give me a little time. Let me work out a plan." He gave Pinch a quick look and then away again. "I'm the one who's been in there, not any of you. Maybe I can figure out something." He glanced at Pinch again. Suggesting that they follow his plan, rather than Pinch's, was dangerously close to rebellion. Pinch was four inches taller, stronger, twenty pounds heavier. "I know the lay of the land in there, Pinch doesn't." They ought to see the sense of that.

Pinch stared at Chipper, his eyes narrowed, his head bent forward, his fists clenched at his sides. "I told yez all Chipper was gettin' too big for his pants. He means to take all them there jewels and gold for himself. Wouldn't surprise me none if he already done it, takin' it out little by little and hidin' it somewheres. That's why he don't want to let us in on it."

"That's not true," Chipper shouted. He looked around for a brick or a piece of metal he could hit Pinch with if Pinch lunged. "I haven't taken anything out of there. She'd have caught me." He looked at the others.

They shifted uneasily. "I don't think Chipper would do that, Pinch," Annie said.

"Still," Jabber said. "Chipper's got to do what Pinch says. That's the way of it in our gang."

Chipper put his hands on his hips and puffed out his cheeks. At least he wouldn't have to fight Pinch just yet. "You won't be in there two minutes before somebody wakes up and hollers for the cops. You're—we're all going to jail."

But Shad and Annie had seen the sense of what Chipper had said, had persuaded Pinch to hold off a little until Chipper could explore the house a little more. Chipper promised that he would do so, and having made the promise, he would have to do it. He could see that somehow, step by step, the decision was being made for him. There had to be a way out. Twice more he went over to Mulberry Street, down the damp little alleyway into the forgotten storage room to talk to the coin. Seeing the coin, of course, reminded Chipper of his ma, and that got him to thinking about Charles Sibley. He liked the idea that the two might have been friends. Oh, it was far-fetched, that he knew; but still, he liked imagining that Charles Sibley had come down to the Bowery to go to the theater, and his ma had been walking home from her job on Prince Street, carrying a bag of potatoes or something; and a potato had rolled out of the bag just as she was crossing the Bowery; and before she could bend down, this goodlooking swell had swooped over to pick up the potato; their eyes had met and instantly they had known they were meant for each other. Something like that, anyway. Chipper knew the whole idea was silly, but he liked thinking about it, anyway, and sometimes he let himself do it.

Chipper had even taken the trouble to go to the library near to where he used to live on Mulberry Street to look up the word "scarab." He had not been in the library for some while, but he used to go as a child to return books occasionally and wasn't afraid to go. A scarab turned out to be a beetle, or the image of a beetle, "much used among the ancient Egyptians as a symbol, seal, amulet, or the like." Chipper liked the idea that he might have something to do with the ancient Egyptians, and he memorized the definition—although to be sure, his knowledge of ancient Egypt was scant. Someday he would study all about them.

In the meantime he had his promise to the Midnight Rats to fulfill. He thought about it hard for a while. He would at least get a look around the rest of the house and perhaps something would occur to him, some way they could steal a few things with nobody getting caught.

So the next time he was having tea he asked Miss Sibley about the turret. "Is the room inside round, like the outside?"

"Charles liked to play in that room on rainy days when he

couldn't go out. It was mostly used for storage, but Charles moved the things around and made a play space for himself. He would pretend it was a medieval castle and fight off the enemy trying to climb into the castle. Unfortunately, once he fired some arrows out into Fifth Avenue. They were blunt-ended, but still, it caused quite a commotion."

"Could I see it?" She'd never said much about Charles Sibley, and Chipper was eager to know more. Charles was sort of his father, after all. "I've never seen a round room before."

So they went on up the wide stairs that rose from the front hall. It was his first time above the ground floor. Here was another hall, with more crystal chandeliers, walls of pictures, mostly photographs of people, and doors leading here and there. Which was her bedroom? Pinch would certainly insist on knowing that. One of the doors was half open. Through it he could see a piece of a bureau and a sofa. "Is that where you sleep?" he asked. He felt hot and guilty.

"Yes," she said, not even turning around. She went on down the hall, up another flight of stairs to the third floor. She opened the door. They stepped inside. The room was indeed round, with a large window that looked out onto Fifth Avenue. Stacked haphazardly around were large trunks, a dressmaker's dummy, a couple of rough shelves of books, boxes and barrels containing Chipper did not know what. He could see that some of the barrels and boxes had been pushed away from the area by the window. He crossed the room and looked out. Down below was the sidewalk with its pedestrians, and then Fifth Avenue with its carriages and wagons passing by in both directions.

"How old was he when he shot the arrows out?"

"About your age, I suppose. He liked shooting his arrows at things he shouldn't have. He was a wonderful boy. Full of mischief but not a bad boy. When he was little he liked climbing up on things and jumping off, shouting that he was flying."

Chipper could see Charles Sibley leaning out the window with his bow, shooting arrows at the carriages moving up and down Fifth Avenue. Suddenly he wished that he had been there, too, and that he and his friend Charles had played knights in a castle and had caused a commotion together. He turned away from the window. "Did he have a lot of friends?"

She smiled. "A boy who likes to get into mischief always has a lot of friends. To be sure, a good many of them were his cousins. You met one of them, William Hodge, the lawyer." She paused. "He was my brother, Chipper. Did you know that?"

"I wasn't sure."

"Well, he was. He was ten years younger than I. Our mother died when he was little, and then our father died, too. Charles was only eight and I had to take over." She paused and smiled. "We had wonderful times together."

It was finally coming out. "What happened to him?"

She frowned and gazed out the window. "It was a great tragedy. So much promise coming to nothing. He had trouble growing up. It's one thing to be mischievous at the age of eight. It's another to be mischievous at twenty. I suppose it was because he lost his mother so young. He was only two. I was twelve, and had had her for all that time." She looked at Chipper. "But of course you lost a mother when you were young, too, didn't you?"

"I was six. I can remember her real well."

"It makes a difference. Charles always said he couldn't remember her, and I suppose that was it. He did badly at school. He wouldn't study; he said it was dull. Even as a teenager he began seeing—how shall I put it?—people who were not good for him. At fifteen he decided that he was the man of the house and wouldn't take orders from an older sister, even though I was his legal guardian. It was a difficult time. We stopped being friends. He wanted me to give him money to spend as he wished, and I wouldn't. He was destroying himself with it. Of course, people gather around wealthy, reckless young men to see what they can get out of them. They encouraged him in his ways."

Was his ma one of those who had encouraged Charles Sibley in his ways? Well, if Charles Sibley and his ma had been friends, she hadn't got anything from him, that was obvious. Had Patcher encouraged Charles Sibley in his ways? Chipper wasn't quite sure how old Dick Patcher was, but he clearly must have been just a boy when Charles had been found floating in the East River. Patcher couldn't have done much toward encouraging Charles Sibley in his ways, assuming he had even known him.

"Did they get a lot of his money?"

"He didn't really have a great deal of money. It was tied

up in a trust." She looked at him quizzically. "Do you know what a trust is?"

"Not exactly."

"It means that money, or a house, a business, anything, is put aside under the control of somebody else. I was the trustee. Charles would have come into the money, the house, the businesses, and so forth when he was twenty-five. But he didn't live."

He still wasn't getting enough to add one plus one— that is, his ma and Charles Sibley—to make him. "I heard he drowned."

She looked at him. "Who told you that? Mr. Patcher?"

He was about to lie out of habit, when it occurred to him that there was no reason to. Why lie to her? "Yes. Dick Patcher told me."

She was silent for a minute, reflecting. Then she said, "Did Mr. Patcher tell you he was the one who found the body?"

Chipper was astonished. The idea had never occurred to him. "What?" he said.

"He was only a boy. Younger than you are now. He said he had been swimming at dusk and had seen something out in the river. He dragged the body in." She shuddered, closed her eyes, and put her hand onto the top of a barrel to steady herself. But Chipper hardly noticed, because it was occurring to him that if Patcher had found the body, he might also have found the ring. Did he still have it? Might he have sold it? Surely Miss Sibley would have paid him plenty for it. Of course, if Patcher had been nine or ten at the time, he might not have had any sense of what it was worth and sold it to a pawnbroker for a few dollars. He was determined he would ask Patcher.

Miss Sibley straightened herself, crossed her arms over her chest, and gave Chipper a sad smile. "It's difficult for me to talk about it even now. But you ought to know."

With a sudden shock, Chipper saw that Miss Sibley did in fact believe that he was Charles Sibley's son. He had been wrong about it; they had deceived her. He glanced at her and then away. He couldn't look at her. It was all lies. Patcher had had the ring at least long enough to remember what it looked like. He had taken it off the corpse, perhaps had kept it, but probably had sold it. Possibly he'd been afraid of offering it to Miss Sibley, who might have gone to the police about it. It didn't matter: It was all lies, and Chipper had been part of the game to get her to believe them. He felt dirty and sick of himself. And on top of it he'd got her to show him the round room so he could spy out where she kept her jewelry. He was worthless. Why hadn't he told her the truth somewhere along the line?

He knew one thing: He couldn't lie to her anymore. Despite himself, they had become friends. She had been kinder to him than anyone ever had, except his ma, and so far as he could see she didn't want anything from him, except to let her be his friend. How could he help liking her? He had come to see something else, too. Miss Sibley did not really understand what it was like to be a street boy, did not understand that when you were hungry you could not call for food, when you were cold you could not call for warmth, but in such cases simply had to suffer and endure. But he saw that she had, in her own way, suffered, just as he had—seen her parents die, watched her little brother go bad, die a nasty death, and found herself alone in a grand house with vast wealth. She, too, had suffered, and he would not add to that suffering. Suddenly he wanted to protect her.

What was he going to do? Tell her the truth? Tell her that the whole thing had been a pack of lies? It was what he ought to do, but he wasn't going to hurt her. Whatever the case, he was going to put an end to the deception as soon as he could. After that he would go away and cause her no more pain. It would be painful enough as it was. What about Dick Patcher? He was going to be a problem all right. Patcher, Chipper knew, was dangerous: He had seen the sudden, cold rage come over him when Pinch had tried to cross him, and he knew that Patcher had come close to doing Pinch some real damage. Patcher was cool and collected, but he could be dangerous, too. What was Chipper going to do about him? He didn't know.

However, she was still caught up in the past and didn't notice his silence. "They said it was suicide. It wasn't. I knew Charles. He enjoyed things too much for that. I believe it was an accident." Her face got cold and still, as if she were determined to feel the horror no longer. "No doubt he had been drinking." She shook herself. "Enough of this unpleasant subject. Let's go down to tea."

*　*　*

They had tea and cake and she talked about happier things, trying to shake off the dark shadow that Charles had cast over them both, for different reasons. After a while she began to talk about her cottage in Newport, Rhode Island. "It's very pleasant. It's right on the beach; we have sailboats and things, and there are always children around, cousins, old family friends. Charles was very fond of sailing. He was good at it, but he would sail too fast, heeling the boat over until water came over the gunnels. He was always tipping over."

In Chipper's mind, a cottage was a tiny house with a straw roof, like the ones he had seen in the books his ma had read to him when he was little. He had difficulty picturing Miss Sibley living in a place like the one inhabited by Hansel and Gretel, and even more difficulty envisioning her sweeping off the front step with a broom made of twigs. *Cottage*, he decided, must be just an expression. "I didn't know about that," he said. He sat there, filling with sadness.

She raised her teacup to her lips and looked at him over it. "Customarily I spend the summer there. We always have, going back to my grandfather's time." She paused. "How would you like to go up with me?"

He knew instantly that she was asking him because she was trying to cast off the dark shadow of Charles Sibley, which Chipper had himself called up through his curiosity to know more about him. He didn't seem to be able to do anything right anymore. Everything he did hurt somebody—Miss Sibley of course, but Patcher, Pinch, and the rest of them, too. What could he tell her?

"Does the idea upset you, Chipper?" she said anxiously.

He didn't want to hurt her any more. "No, no," he said hastily. "I would like to. Only . . ." Only what? I'd rather stay in New York and rob you, Miss Sibley?

She nodded sympathetically. "Yes, it'll be very different for you. Meeting a lot of new young people from a different world. We'll have to get you some new clothes, but I'll enjoy that."

"Yes," he said.

"And your manners want some improving."

There was nothing he could say but yes. "I'd like it a lot, Miss Sibley." But he wouldn't be going.

Twelve

William Hodge sat behind his desk, staring out the window at the long view across New York harbor. On the desk before him lay a legal paper filled with *wherefores* and *therewiths*, and signed at the bottom with the small, cramped signature of Millie O'Connell, and the larger, bolder signature of Bert O'Connell, which appeared, from the ink blotches, to have been labored over. At the bottom was a notary's stamp and an embossed seal.

Elizabeth Sibley sat stiffly on the sofa, her chin pulled back, her hands gripping the purse in her lap. "I don't believe it," she said. "Where did you get it?"

"Your beloved cousin Frederick Sibley provided me with it. He has kept a second copy."

"Frederick was never any use from childhood," Elizabeth snapped. "He whined all the time. Even as a boy he couldn't be trusted. Charles had to put up with him as a cousin, but he used to do an imitation of Frederick whining that was regrettably like. Frederick's word is worthless."

William Hodge nodded. He wished people wouldn't always get emotional about things, but he had long since accepted the fact that they did and had become used to it. You had to bring them around to reality. "That may or may not be the case. Nonetheless, Frederick has got these close relatives of the boy to swear that Charles was not the father. That's going to be difficult to get around."

"He paid them. He has a great deal to gain by it. Surely a court will see that."

William Hodge nodded to show sympathy to her point of view. "I have no doubt that he gave them some money to elicit their cooperation. People like that would not go to any trouble just to oblige Frederick. But it doesn't follow that they are lying."

"I know they're lying. People like that would say anything for money. You have no idea how much a few dollars would mean to them, William."

"That may also be true. But Frederick has been assiduous. He's collected papers. The husband, O'Connell, was born in County Cork and came here when he was twelve with an older brother, but the wife and the boy's mother were both born in New York. There are birth records for them. He's also managed to get the boy's school records."

"Frederick appears to have spent a good deal of money eliciting people's cooperation, as you so delicately put it."

William did not respond to that. "Frederick's tied it all together. He'll be able to show in court from birth records that the mother and Mrs. O'Connell were sisters. He'll show that the mother and the boy lived on Mulberry Street, and that the sister and her husband lived on Crosby Street three blocks away. He'll be able to show from the death certificate that the brother-in-law, Bert O'Connell, took delivery of the mother's body; he'll be able to show from the school records that the boy lived with the O'Connells for a period of years. It would appear from all of this that Chipper's mother, Emmy Carey, as she was called, was on good terms with her sister, Millie O'Connell. Nothing the boy has ever said would contradict that. Any court will find it difficult to believe that the O'Connells didn't know who Chipper's father was. Their testimony will almost certainly stand up in court." He paused and laid his hands flat on the desk. "I think you have to face that, Elizabeth."

He watched her shift sideways on the sofa to look out the window at the ships leaving white wakes in the blue water below.

"God damn Frederick," she said softly. "God damn him."

As well as William Hodge knew Elizabeth, this strong language startled him. As a girl she had been something of a tomboy, a hoyden, and had used slang as the boys did, but he had never before heard her use these words. She had been foolish and had been blunt, but even so, he felt a little wintery pity for her.

"I'm sorry, Elizabeth. But it's better that you know. He'll get nothing from the estate. It'll go to Frederick."

"Frederick. It's unbearable." She put her hands over her face. "Frederick living in my house, the house I was born in, the house I expect to die in. I can't bear it, William."

"You want it too much, Elizabeth. I learned a long time ago that it's best not to want things too much."

170

She was silent. Then she said. "It's all lies. What did they say the father's name was?"

William looked at the paper. "Bill Jones."

"Bill Jones," she said bitterly. "They weren't even clever about it. You know perfectly well that Frederick paid them off."

William said nothing, but began to twirl the letter opener on the desk top. It came from caring too much, he thought. "Elizabeth, it isn't going to matter what I think or what you think. It'll matter what a court thinks. You'd need to have evidence that there was collusion, perjury, whatever."

"No court will ever convince me that Chipper isn't the boy. I'll do what I want for him."

William shook his head. "You must remember, Elizabeth, that most of the money isn't yours. You only hold it in trust for others, in this case, as it works out, Frederick. If you start spending the money on Chipper, Frederick might with reason go to court to stop you." He remembered that Elizabeth didn't like the spinning letter opener, and leaned back in his chair. "Oh, if you took him into the house, fed him, bought clothes for him, perhaps even had him tutored a little, there couldn't be any objection. You've got some money of your own, of course. But if you started sending him away to expensive schools and colleges, bought him a law practice, set him up in business, that would be another matter. You could, I suppose, eventually find him a job in one of your concerns—send him out west to the copper mine to learn the business, perhaps. But how long do you think Frederick would keep him when he took over?

Frederick, you may be assured, will do nothing for him. He'll suddenly find himself destitute."

"Frederick," she said, her lips rolling as if she had taken a mouthful of ashes. "It's unbearable."

William leaned forward over the desk. "I know you don't want to hear this, Elizabeth, but for the boy's own sake, it might be best for you to apprentice him to a trade—the printing trades, perhaps, like engraving, book-binding. His grandfather was in the printing trades. He'd never be wealthy, but he'd always be comfortable. Given his background, it's only realistic. Can't you see what an odd fish he'd be if you sent him to a good school? You know what boys are like. They'll pillory him. Get him a trade, Elizabeth. It'll be of real value to him."

The room was quiet. Then she said, "He looks so much like Charles. You said so yourself, William. He's the image of Charles."

She was begging him, William realized. But there was really nothing he could do for her, even if he had wanted to. "Yes, I grant that, Elizabeth. But after all, people do resemble other people. It's a common occurrence."

"The name, William. Chipper can be a nickname for Charles."

"That has occurred to me. You can't make very much of it, Elizabeth. Even if his name were Charles, you couldn't make very much of it."

"But the ring," she said loudly. "He knew about the ring. He described it exactly without being prompted."

William shrugged. "There are a hundred possible explanations. This man Patcher may have met Charles in one of those Bowery dives. The ring may have been common knowledge. A wealthy young man who travels in those circles gets talked about. A lot of people might have known about the ring."

"You're saying that Patcher described it to Chipper."

William shrugged. "I'm not saying anything. Elizabeth, please try to remember that almost all of this is speculation. We're only guessing about a lot of it. All I'm saying is that Patcher *could* have coached Chipper. I'm not saying that he did."

"No," she said loudly. "Not Chipper. I know him too well. We're—friends now. You'll never get me to believe that Chipper concocted the story."

For a long while nobody said anything. Then she said, "You don't accept that."

"No," he said softly. "I believe you're being made a fool of by swindlers. Oh, I don't know how much the boy is involved. Perhaps he's an innocent dupe." He paused and started spinning the letter opener again. This time he didn't stop. "Probably the truth lies somewhere in between. I know you, Elizabeth. I was the younger cousin and you and Charles were rather scornful of me. Even so, I don't want to see you made a fool of, particularly when it may prove expensive." He paused again, giving the letter opener a last spin. "To be truthful, Elizabeth, I am not entirely convinced that Frederick is necessarily the best person to entrust the estate to, if I may put it that way. As you know, his father showed poor business judgment on more than one occasion, and Frederick hasn't done any better. I would not be disappointed if it fell into other hands. I can go with you that far. But I don't think Chipper is the ideal choice, either." He looked at her. "Please, Elizabeth, don't go any further with this without at least letting me know what you plan to do."

Dick Patcher prided himself on the fact that, unlike many of his friends in similar businesses, he did not simply plunge from day to day, grabbing at whatever opportunities came along and spending the profit as quickly as possible. Patcher believed in thinking things through, in looking to the future, in knowing who your friends are.

In line with this, he had taken the trouble to make a study of Pinch Mulligan's mind. Patcher had concluded that Pinch was not going to let Chipper Carey move freely in and out of a household filled with valuables without trying to get his hands on some of those valuables. Patcher had also concluded that Pinch's methods of obtaining some of these valuables would not be subtle nor that he would be patient about it.

Dick Patcher had also made a study of Chipper Carey's mind. Chipper, he had concluded, was a somewhat more complex piece of work than Pinch. He was, Patcher feared, inclined to be sentimental about things. Like William Hodge, Dick Patcher did not like to see an excess of sentimentality come crowding into business affairs. He much preferred dealing with people who he knew for certain would lie, would cheat, would steal, for he understood such people. Patcher was not entirely sure he knew how Chipper's mind worked. But he sensed that Chipper might grow sentimental about Elizabeth Sibley. That, of course, would never do. As a consequence, Patcher had made a point of meeting with Chipper every week, more or less, just to make sure Chipper kept his eye screwed tightly on the primary object, which was money, rather than to let it wander off in the direction of affection, friendliness, good fellowship, all of which Dick Patcher considered serious flaws of character. A man never got anywhere in life by being a good fellow.

Both Patcher and Chipper had reasons for wanting to keep their festive weekly conclaves from Pinch and the Midnight Rats generally. As a consequence, on this occasion they were meeting at Cloake's, a restaurant on Spring Street by the Hudson River, a good distance from the Rats' usual stomping grounds, eating lamb stew and drinking cold punch. Chipper was always glad of a good meal. This time the occasion was not going to be entirely pleasant, however, for Chipper had to begin breaking the news to Dick Patcher that he couldn't go on deceiving Miss Sibley any longer. The whole thing scared him a good deal. Chipper's idea, then, was to slowly make it seem that Miss Sibley was not going to do anything for Chipper except feed him tea and tarts; perhaps gradually Patcher would see that the game was lost and give it up.

Patcher took a sip of punch. "So, Chipper, how's yez gettin' along with the old lady?"

"I don't think she's so old. I think she's around forty-five."

"With women," Patcher said, "allus add on five years. At least. Maybe ten in this here case."

He was not going to let Patcher call her a liar. "She didn't tell me. I figured it out from things she said."

Patcher ignored that. "They're vain creatures, women is," he said in a philosophic manner. "Vain as dogs, in a manner of speaking. Play up to their vanity and you can allus bring 'em around. Play up to their vanity, Chipper." He gave Chipper a look. "I 'spect yer doin' that already without me telling yez. I 'spect yer tellin' her how kind and generous she is. Especially generous. I 'spect yez tell her how generous she is every time she passes yez a slice of cake. I 'spect yez can't hardly get the cake into yer mouth before yez says, 'Miss Sibley, I never seen nobody like yez for generousness. Yez must have been born a saint.'" Patcher kept his eyes on Chipper. "I 'spect yez been doin' that right along."

Playing up to Miss Sibley's vanity was precisely what Chipper had determined he would not do. He could not say that to Patcher, however. He struggled to think of something to say. "I don't think she wants me to praise her all the time. She isn't that kind of a person." That, it seemed to Chipper, was quite true. Miss Sibley, he figured, would only be annoyed if he harped on her virtues all the time.

Patcher shook his head sadly. "I'm surprised, Chipper. I really am. Here I took yez for smart as a whip, and yez ain't even done what anybody with half a brain would of thought of. They're vain creatures. Yez gotta flatter 'em constant."

It was clear to Chipper that Patcher was wrong about this. That was the difference between Patcher and him: Patcher had never known anyone but people like himself, where Chipper had known two—his ma and now Miss Sibley. The idea that he might know something that Dick Patcher didn't emboldened Chipper. He said, "I know her better than you do. She isn't that way."

Patcher narrowed his eyes warily. "Maybe yez does and maybe yez don't," he said finally. He took a sip of the cold punch. "She ain't said nothin' about yez moving in with her yet?"

"No. She isn't going to do that. We're just friends."

Patcher shook his head a little wearily. "There's some fellas what couldn't see their chances if they was to fall over them, so to put it. Here I got it fixed so this here rich lady's gone sweet on yez, feedin' yez cakes and pie like there wasn't no end to 'em, and yez can't see the chanct yez got layin' in front of yer face, in a manner of speakin'." He shook his head again. "Maybe I made a mistake. Maybe I should of handed it over to another boy." He bent forward to take in a large spoonful of stew, but he kept his eyes on Chipper.

Chipper saw his opportunity. "Maybe you should have. I don't think she believes I'm the son of Charles Sibley."

Dick Patcher stared at Chipper hard. "What makes yez think that?"

He thought quickly. "She showed me this picture she has of him. A big painting. She said we looked alike but it was probably just a coincidence."

Patcher cocked his head. "Didn't yez say nothin' about that there ring? Didn't yez bring that to her attention, so to put it?"

"She knows all about that. Why do I have to bring it to her attention?"

Patcher went on staring at Chipper for a moment. Then he said slowly, "Yez wouldn't be thinkin' of double-crossing old Dick Patcher, would yez, Chipper?'

Chipper realized that he had gone too far. "No, no. It isn't that. I think she's suspicious of it. Wouldn't you be, Dick?" It was a reasonable idea. He hoped Patcher would buy it.

Patcher looked off up at the tin ceiling and then went on in his measured way. "For if I figured yez was double-crossin' me, Chipper, yer name would be mud, so to put it." Suddenly he looked down, reached across the table and grabbed Chipper by the front of his shirt. "Mud, Chipper." He gave the shirt a jerk, pulling Chipper up against the edge of the table. "Mud."

He let go and leaned back, his breath coming hard. In a low whisper, Chipper said, "Dick, I wasn't double-crossing you. I think she's suspicious."

"Yez make sure that she stops being suspicious, so to put it. Yez understand me?"

"Yes." Chipper whispered.

"Now I got one more thing to raise with yez. When's Pinch Mulligan plannin' on bustin' into the old lady's place?"

Chipper jerked upright, as if pulled from above by

strings. "I . . . I." Quick, think of something. "He's . . . I don't know if he's planning anything," he finally got out.

"I figure he is. Pinch ain't one to let a chanct like this gallop on by, in a manner of speakin'. When's it to be? This week? Next week?" He went on watching Chipper carefully.

Anything he said would be wrong. But he couldn't sit there staring at Patcher. "I don't know when."

"Well, I do, Chipper. Yez can tell Pinch that there old lady is me meat, not his. Yez can tell him I'm keepin' an eye on him, and if he goes within half a mile of that there place I'm gonna bust him in half. And that ain't no manner of speakin', neither."

But of course Chipper couldn't tell Pinch that Patcher would break him in half if he robbed Miss Sibley's house. Pinch would simply assume that Chipper had double-crossed the gang and had told Patcher about the plan. It would be a serious charge to answer for. In fact, they would run him out of the gang.

He was trapped. There was no way out. Either he double-crossed Patcher or he double-crossed the Midnight Rats, and no matter what he did he would double-cross Miss Sibley, the only one of them who didn't want something from him. Well, better to double-cross Patcher than the gang. That meant going ahead with the robbery. He remembered what Miss Sibley had said: She had so much, and they had so little. They had been his people long before he had met Miss Sibley. He had to choose, and they were his choice.

Then he would have to flee, run for it, leave the Bowery, go to some other part of the city to start over again somehow, someway. He would ache with loneliness, that he knew. But what else could he do?

Thirteen

He would have to go up to the house one more time, obviously, in order to make up some sort of plan for them and unlock a window. He'd never believed in Pinch's plan, and there was a good chance that it wouldn't work. They weren't going to get all those diamonds and pearls that Pinch had built up in their minds. Chipper assumed that Miss Sibley had jewels; rich people always did. She never wore any to amount to anything, he'd noticed—never wore a big diamond ring, a pearl necklace, usually nothing much by way of jewelry beyond a pin on her shirt or a brooch where her dress buttoned up at the throat. He also assumed that she kept whatever jewelry she had in her room—that seemed obvious. But where, he had no idea and didn't intend to find out.

No, about all they could expect to take out of the house would be silver candlesticks and candy dishes, the silver coffee service that sat on the dining room sideboard, perhaps some clocks. They'd wake somebody up pretty quickly, and soon enough the police would be arriving. From an economic viewpoint, Chipper knew, the whole thing was silly. He had only the vaguest idea of Miss Sibley's wealth, but he knew that she would hardly miss what the Midnight Rats would steal.

Drawing up a map wouldn't be hard. He already knew where a lot of things were. The Simon Willard clock on the sitting room mantelpiece was supposed to be valuable because of Simon Willard, whoever he was, and was small enough for one of them to manage. There were the six tall silver candlesticks on the dining room table, there was the set of silver teaspoons Miss Sibley had shown him once because they had been made by Paul Revere—Chipper had at least known who Paul Revere was, there was the cut glass punch bowl on the sideboard, which they were bound to break getting it out of the house. When he was there he would make notes in his head of a few other things.

Getting a window unlocked would be harder. It couldn't be one along the front of the house, lit by the streetlights on Fifth Avenue. The back of the house was visible from the stable, where the coachman and the stable boy slept on the second floor. Safest probably would be one of the parlor windows, which was on the north side of the house and faced into the gravel drive leading around back to the stable. If they went along the drive down the side of the house twenty feet or so, they'd be in shadows and fairly well concealed from the avenue. He'd have a look at it when he was there.

So then there was nothing to do but wait. More and more, Chipper felt swallowed up in bitterness. He wished he'd never met Patcher, never gone to tea with Miss Sibley. He was sick of the gang, and he spent as much time as he could wandering alone around his part of the city, sitting on East River wharfs, watching the bustle of ships being loaded and unloaded, with the streets full of barrows, carts, wagons, shouting, noise; walking slowly up Mulberry Street, through the pushcarts and the housewives crowded around, to stare at the tenement where had lived as a child, thinking of his ma; sitting in Washington Square where, years before he had been born, another boy had chased up flurries of pigeons. Well, he needn't think about that anymore.

He had, of course, to make it look as if everything were normal, and he made an effort to joke around with the gang, or talk about the usual things, like whether Jim Corbett was really a better boxer than John L. Sullivan. Chipper made a point of getting into such discussions.

But Annie noticed. One evening, when the two of them had wandered off up the Bowery to see if something might turn up, she said, "What's the matter with yez, Chipper?"

"What?" he said, looking at her, startled. "Why do you think something's the matter with me?"

"Oh, yez been kind of gloomy for a while. Don't have nothin' to say for yerself. We been walking for fifteen minutes and you ain't hardly said a word."

In the past he might have just said that he was feeling sick or something, but he was learning that if you went close to the truth it was likely to sound believable. "I'm worried about this heist in the old lady's house. They won't go easy on us if we get caught. It isn't like heisting a sack of spuds from a pushcart."

"What makes yez think we're gonna get caught?"

"Suppose somebody's awake and hears footsteps downstairs. Anything can happen."

"Chipper, yez got to look on the bright side more. Don't think of somebody awaking up. Think of all them jewels and stuff we're going to have."

"I don't know if that's the smartest way to think. Maybe it's better to think of the problems you could run into." She stared at him. "I think there's something else wrong, Chipper."

He wished he could tell her. He desperately wanted to talk to somebody about it. It would be such a relief to tell somebody what he was feeling, even though that wouldn't, in reality, change anything. But he couldn't tell—couldn't tell Annie, couldn't tell Miss Sibley, couldn't tell Dick Patcher, Pinch, any of them, for they all had a stake in it, something important for them to win or lose. And Chipper held the key to their winning and losing. "Let's talk about something else, Annie. I'll try to cheer up."

Then the day came, a warm May day of the kind that makes you want to be outside. At the appointed hour he went up Fifth Avenue to the house with the round room and the stained-glass cranes standing in their marshes on either side of the door. However, he walked a little past the door to where the gravel drive began at the sidewalk and looked down along the side of the house. The bottoms of the parlor windows were a good six feet above the ground, but Pinch would be able to reach up and grab hold of the sill if Chipper opened the window enough for Pinch to slide his fingers in. On the opposite side of the drive, away from the house, was a long row of tall forsythia bushes. At night the ground under the spreading forsythia branches would be in deep shadows: A fair number of the gang could hide there, unseen from either Fifth Avenue or the stable perhaps a hundred feet farther back.

So that was that, and Chipper went into the house.

They had tea in the parlor. Chipper found it hard to force down his cake, but he knew Miss Sibley would find it strange if he didn't eat as he usually did. Actually, she was busy talking about the summer excursion to Newport, and perhaps would not notice what he ate. However, Chipper had learned that Miss Sibley tended to notice things. He was glad, nonetheless, that she was doing most of the talking, so he could sit quiet in his misery.

Nonetheless, as she talked he took an occasional casual look at the wall with the windows which looked out on the gravel drive. In the center of the wall was the yellow silk sofa, and over the sofa the by now familiar portrait of the boy on the stone bench with his ruffled shirt, the watch fob with its gold ornament, the ring with the green stone in it. The window latch on top of the bottom sash was a little above Chipper's reach; but if he stood on the right end of the sofa he would be able to reach across and snap the latch open. It would take ten seconds, or a little longer, allowing for a couple of seconds to slide the sash up enough for Pinch to slip his fingers through.

"I think we'll arrange about getting you some summer clothes, Chipper. You'll need a bathing suit, of course. Do you know how to swim at all?"

"Some," he said. "We swim in the rivers on hot days."

But he wasn't going to need a bathing suit.

"We can have you instructed in any case. There's a man who gives the children swimming lessons. Boating lessons, too, I suppose. I haven't paid much attention to it for years, not since Charles was a boy. I'll ask my cousin May. She has children about your age. You'll meet them, of course." He wouldn't meet them, nor would he have boating lessons. He wished she'd shut up about it. It was only making things worse. He tried to think of a way to get her onto another subject.

Suddenly she stopped talking and looked at him with her shrewd eye. "You're rather quiet today, Chipper. Is something bothering you?"

"No, no," he said quickly. "Nothing's bothering me."

She watched him for a moment. Chipper flushed, sick of himself. Miss Sibley leaned forward and touched his forehead with the back of her hand. "You feel hot," she said. "I shouldn't wonder if you're coming down with something. It's the change of seasons. You need something— liver pills, perhaps." She rose and walked out of the parlor, her heels clicking on the marble tiles of the hall.

Chipper stood and walked swiftly across the room, as if intending to look at the portrait. If she caught him on the sofa he could say that he'd climbed up to get a closer look at the ring. In truth, looking at the picture had always given him a curious feeling, as if he'd suddenly discovered that he had a twin he'd never heard of before but who would now become an important part of his life. It was eerie, looking at that brown hair, the lips, the eyes so like his own.

For a moment he listened for the sound of heels clicking. There was silence. Quickly he scuffed his shoes on the carpet to remove any dirt, so as not to leave traces on the yellow silk upholstery, and stepped up onto the sofa seat next to the right-hand arm. He stretched his arm out to reach for the window catch. In doing so his face was pulled close to the picture, so that the shiny gold ornament on the watch fob was directly in front of him. He had never seen the picture this close, and for just a second he let his eyes rest on the fob.

And then he stood in astonishment on the sofa, his heart pounding, his eyes wide, the world swinging upside down around him. His mouth fell open and he gasped. The gold on the watch fob was not just a simple design or decoration. It was instead a gold coin with the image of Queen Victoria on it, inscribed with a large, decorative, scroll-like C. There could not be two such coins in the world.

Then he heard the click of heels on the marble tiles of the hall. With a swift motion he snapped open the window latch and shoved the frame upward a couple of inches. He had just time enough to jump down from the sofa and stand looking at the picture before Miss Sibley came back into the parlor.

"I often wonder," she said, "what you think when you look at that picture."

He stood before her stunned and bewildered, his mind clogged so that he hardly knew what he was saying. "I think he's my father," he whispered.

She stood facing him, holding a small pill jar in her

hands. "I'm glad you've come to believe that, Chipper. I think he is, too." Then she said, "Chipper, you really don't look well. You're as white as a sheet. I want you to lie down and rest."

He shook himself as if he were trying to pull himself from a heavy sleep. "No, no," he gasped. "There's something I have to do."

"What can be so important? I knew something was troubling you."

"I can't tell you, Miss Sibley. I have to go, I just have to go." He ran out of the parlor and then down the marble tile to the front door.

"Chipper," she cried, running after him. "Chipper, what on earth is the matter?"

"I can't tell you," he threw over his shoulder. "Just have to go." He reached the front door, banged it open and charged through.

"Chipper," she called from the front door. "What ever it is, you can tell me. Just come back."

But already he was racing down the sidewalk, tears flying off his face like rain in the wind.

He found the Midnight Rats under the Brooklyn Bridge, waiting for him. His face was smudged with tears and dirt where he had spent a half hour lying facedown in a dirty alleyway, sobbing. But he had calmed himself and was ready for them. He took out of his pocket a piece of butcher paper he had found in the street and the stub of a pencil he had hunted up in a dump.

"Here's your map," he said. "I got it worked out . . ."

He crouched and smoothed the piece of paper on a packing box slat. Quickly he began to draw. "You come up the driveway here to this window." He drew an X. "The window's unlocked. Shove it up and slip through. Here's the hall here, here's the dining room, here's what she calls the sitting room." He sketched the outlines of the room. "There's a clock here that's supposed to be worth a lot." He made an X. "Here's the silver coffee service. Here are six candlesticks." He went on sketching, making Xs, scribbling names. In five minutes it was done.

There was silence. Then Pinch said, "It don't seem like much. There's gotta be a heap of money layin' around."

"Well, there isn't. I told you a month ago it was a lousy plan and you weren't going to get anything like what you thought out of it."

Pinch gave him a hard look, but he didn't say anything. "Yez certain? I thought them rich people had lots of money laying around."

"Well, they don't. Maybe there's money in the safe. I don't know."

"Where's the safe?"

He jabbed with the pencil stub. "Here. In this office. But there's no way you're going to open a safe without waking everybody up." He gave Pinch a hard look. "You can forget about it, Pinch."

That was obvious. "Where's her jewels? She must have a ton of jewels. All them rich people do."

"I don't know. In her bedroom, I guess. I was never in there."

"Where's it at, her bedroom?"

"Pinch, the minute you go in there with your candle she'll wake up and holler for the servants."

"We got to get them jewels. Three of us'll go in there and hold her down until she gives us the jewels. Stuff something in her mouth so she can't holler."

Chipper stood. "Pinch, if you lay a finger on her, I'm telling you plain, I'm going to kill you."

Pinch hastily stood. His mouth was open in amazement. "Now look here, Chip—"

"I mean it." He looked around at the others. "You all heard me."

"Chipper," Shad said, "Why do you care about that old lady? Pinch's doing it for the gang.'

"I don't belong to the gang anymore," he said.

"Chipper, don't say that," Annie said. She, too, was on her feet. "You can't quit now, not when we're going to be rich."

"You're not going to be rich. You're going to be lucky if you're not in jail."

"Don't listen to him" Pinch said. "He wants to keep that old lady's stuff for himself."

Chipper shrugged. "You can think what you want. I'm quitting. I did what you wanted, unlocked the window, drew the map. I don't owe you anything anymore. I'm quitting." He started to turn away, and then turned back. "Remember what I said, Pinch. Keep your hands off Miss Sibley, I'll kill you if you touch her."

"Chipper, don't quit us," Annie cried.

He turned and started away at a trot.

"Chipper, come back." But already he was across the street and weaving through the carts and wagons rumbling their way toward the ramps of the Brooklyn Bridge.

Fourteen

One thing was clear: He could not trust Pinch to stay out of Miss Sibley's bedroom. Pinch had gotten his mind set on diamonds and jewels, and he was bound to try to get into her bedroom. Chipper was not at all sure that they'd get that far before they woke the household, but they might. He could not possibly let that happen—could not possibly let Pinch, Shad, Jabber, whoever, hold Miss Sibley down in her bed while they searched for the jewels. Especially not when he had unlocked the window for them. He would have to go up there, hide himself somewhere around the grounds by the stable or something, and watch. If he saw a candle moving in her bedroom, he would scream for the coachman, who Chipper knew had a shotgun. He had warned Pinch; it would be his own fault.

So now he had to stay out of the neighborhood and kill some time. Most of it he spent, as the sun set and the lights of the city came on, just wandering up and down the avenues and streets of New York, looking vaguely at the horses, wagons, and carriages crowding the streets, the people rich and poor coming and going, the shops of fruit, clothing, furniture being shuttered.

Finally, when it was fully dark and he figured he could go back to his old neighborhood without being spotted, he went along to Mulberry Street down the damp-smelling alley and into the forgotten storage room. He took the shiny coin out from behind the brick, tossed the brick to the floor, put the coin in his pocket, and went back out to the street again. In order to finally cut himself loose, he would carry the coin over to the East River at the foot of Tenth Street, where Patcher had dragged the body of his father to the wharf, water rolling out of his pockets, spewing out of his mouth. He would throw the coin as far out into the river as he could, and then he would go . . . somewhere he did not know, but anywhere else but here.

He reached the riverside and stood on the rough wooden wharf. A few small boats were tied up, and on one of them a light shone and voices came up from inside. A few people were sitting on the wharf pilings, smoking and enjoying the cool evening air. Nobody paid any attention to Chipper as he walked to the edge of the wharf and stared out into the wide river. A few boats slipped slowly down the current, and across on the other side, the lights of Brooklyn were reflected on the water. He took the sovereign out of his pocket and clenched it in his fist. Then he opened his hand and held it up so the light would catch the shiny gold surface, just to see it one more time. No doubt of it: It was the same gold coin that had once hung from the watch fob of Charles Sibley, that had been painted in the portrait—the same coin that his father had given to his mother and that his mother had given to him. Well, he must have liked her: The sovereign must have meant a good deal to Charles, or else it wouldn't have been in the picture. And he'd given it to Chipper's ma, not some other girlfriend.

Why had she given it to Chipper, when she wouldn't tell him about his father? She had been too proud to ask the Sibleys for anything, he supposed—she had been like that, proud of speaking like a respectable person and reading books. She wouldn't have gone begging to the Sibleys, nor would have wanted him to, either. That might explain why she'd never told him who his father was. But all the same, she'd wanted him to have a part of his father, even though he was dead. Miss Sibley had explained to him that Chipper could be a nickname for Charles.

What would have happened if Charles Sibley had lived? Would he have been a real father to Chipper—taken him to the beach, baseball games? Chipper didn't know; but he decided to believe that he would have. He couldn't see what harm there was in that.

Well, it was over. He raised his arm to throw. As he did so a light flashed across the coin once more, making it blink. He stopped his hand by his ear. He couldn't do it. None of it was the sovereign's fault: Why should it have to spend eternity at the bottom of the East River? He lowered his arm and stared at the coin again. "I'm sorry," he whispered. "I'll keep you."

He now began to walk swiftly and with determination across Bleecker Street, then up Thompson, into Washington Square and then on up Fifth Avenue. He did not go all the way to Twelfth Street, however, but went across to University Place, up University and back to Fifth on Thirteenth, so he could reach the graveled driveway without having to pass in front of the house. The lights in the parlor were off, and the driveway was dark. He slipped up the drive, keeping to the shadows of the forsythia bushes. When he was hidden from the avenue, he dropped to his knees and crawled through the shadows toward the stable. Here he slipped along the side of the stable until he was well hidden in the darkness, smelling the odor of manure, hay, and old wood that the stable gave off.

From this vantage point he could look straight down the driveway to Fifth Avenue. He could also see the windows of Miss Sibley's bedroom on the second floor over the parlor. He would have, he knew, a long time to wait: Pinch would not bring the gang in until two o'clock in the morning or later.

For a long time Chipper lay there, feeling his heart beat, his forehead damp, his hands clammy, dozing, waking, and dozing some more. From time to time he heard church bells ring, but he could never quite be sure what time they were announcing. He simply waited.

Then he heard faint sounds. He raised himself on his elbows and opened his eyes wide. He stared and blinked and stared again. Down in the lights of Fifth Avenue, a small figure scuttled into the dark of the driveway. For a moment Chipper could see vague movement, and then nothing. There was quiet; and in a minute another small figure scuttled in after the first one and disappeared in the shadows of the forsythia along the graveled drive. Then came a third, and a fourth. Clearly, Pinch was disposing his forces along the driveway. He, probably, would go in first, open the window, and the others would scuttle out of the shadows of the forsythia where they were hiding and pile into the house.

Chipper waited, and in a minute a somewhat larger figure appeared at the end of the driveway, hesitated briefly, and then slipped across the sidewalk into the driveway. This figure, however, did not scuttle into the shadows of the forsythia but, instead, moved swiftly down the side of the house to the window Chipper had, at a time that now seemed long ago, unlatched and slid fractionally open. When the figure reached the window it straightened. In the vague light from the street, Chipper could see the arms stretch up, reaching for the bottom of the window sash.

At that moment Chipper saw yet another figure suddenly appear in the patch of light coming from Fifth Avenue. This one was full-size, and Chipper knew at once it was Dick Patcher. Startled, he rose to a crouch. Then there came a loud gunshot, and a cry in the dark. "I warned yez, Pinch. Yer a dead man."

Pinch dropped to his knees in the gravel. Patcher ran toward him. Behind Chipper in the stable a window slammed open and a rough voice shouted, "Who's there? Who's there?"

Chipper rose to his feet, shouting, "Watch out, Dick, watch out." Even as he shouted, out from the shadows of the forsythia bushes came the Midnight Rats. They swarmed all over Dick Patcher. For a moment, as Chipper ran toward them, they appeared to be nothing but a squirming heap, arms and legs waving, bodies twisting. Then from the stable behind Chipper came the heavy thunderclap of the coachman's shotgun. The squirming heap broke apart, and the gang was fleeing down the drive, half dragging, half carrying Pinch. In a moment they were gone. Dick Patcher lay alone on the gravel driveway.

Chipper ran up and knelt beside him. Patcher was motionless except for a convulsive, rapid heaving of his chest as he struggled for breath. His arms were gripped tight across his chest. "Where did they get you, Dick?"

"All over, Chipper. Stabbed here, there, and every-wheres, so to put it." He raised his hand from his chest. "There's this here one, for starts." He sucked in a long breath of air, shuddering. "Oh my, that there one hurts."

"I'll get a doctor."

"Don't trouble yerself none, Chipper. I'm a goner, so to put it. I can't get no air." For a moment he struggled for breath. "Funny how things work out, ain't it, Chipper. Yez is gonna be rich on account of me, and I ain't gonna get none of it."

"Dick, he was really my father. It wasn't a lie."

"That a fact? Yez couldn't of told it from me."

"He was."

Patcher's eyes began to roll back, and once more he struggled for air.

"Dick, have you still got the ring?"

"The ring?"

Patcher's mind was clouding over, Chipper realized. "The ring with the big green stone."

"Oh. Yeah, I got it."

"Dick, why'd you keep it? Why didn't you sell it?"

He sucked in more air. "Was gonna but then yer friend Miss Sibley come around askin' about how the body looked and sech and I figured that there ring might come in handy someday." Patcher was silent, breathing hard. "Yez may as well have it now, Chipper. I buried it in me little plant. The key to the place is in me pocket."

Chipper heard running footsteps on the gravel. The coachman and the stable boy were coming up. Patcher, too, heard the sounds. "I reckon yez figured out it belonged to him?"

"Yes," Chipper said. "I figured it was on his finger when you found him."

"No." Patcher moved his eyes around vaguely as if trying to recollect where he was. He gasped again. "In his pocket." There was a rattle in his throat. "He had sense enough to put it in his pocket when he was—" Suddenly he stopped and gasped again for breath, his chest heaving and shuddering.

The coachman and the stable boy came panting up and bent over to look. Patcher gasped again. "Oh my, it's like I was on fire in there, in a manner of speakin', Chipper." Then a gush of air rolled out of him, his eyes went blank, his muscles relaxed, and he lay still.

It had taken Frederick Sibley four days to get an appointment with his cousin, the lawyer William Hodge. Hodge, understandably, had been busy attending to the

198

difficulty Elizabeth Sibley had got herself into. There had been a lot of trouble keeping it out of the newspapers, just to begin with. Bribing reporters was never a problem, but there were so many of them and you had to make sure you bribed them all.

Now Frederick was sitting on the sofa in the office with its splendid view of New York harbor.

"William," he said. "You've seen the O'Connells' affidavit. Yes, of course, there's the sovereign. I recognize a jury might give that some credence. But the affidavit . . ."

William shook his head. Frederick was desperate. It was going to be a very painful morning for his cousin. "Frederick, I'm afraid there's more. Chipper got the key out of this man Patcher's pocket. Elizabeth knew that the police would padlock Patcher's place, so by three o'clock in the morning she had collected four Pinkerton men, gone down to Patcher's rooming house, and let herself in. They found a plant in a flowerpot on Patcher's dresser and dumped it out. There was the ring, wrapped in a piece of oilcloth."

"But there you are, William. That clinches it. Patcher had the ring all along. We know he found the body. Undoubtedly he took the ring at that time. Chipper's mother never had it. Chipper's been lying about it all along. Can't Elizabeth see that?"

William shrugged. "We don't know that Patcher took the ring from the body. I've been thinking about that. I wanted to know how a court of law might think. There are a lot of ways Patcher could have gotten hold of the ring: got it from the mother, got it from the O'Connells, saw it in a pawn shop and realized what it was. Bought it, stole it. Perhaps was given it by the mother for some reason. We can't assume it was on the body."

Frederick shook his head firmly. "Those are all far-fetched inventions. Surely a jury would believe that Patcher got the ring from the body."

William nodded. "They might, of course. There's no telling." he paused. "Regrettably, Frederick, Elizabeth found something else in that flowerpot. An affidavit signed by the O'Connells stating that Chipper's father was not Charles Sibley, but somebody else."

"And?" Frederick said. "We knew that."

"Not anymore. This time they swore that the father's name was not Bill Jones, either. It was Henry Smith."

Frederick Sibley sat stock-still as the implications of this fact rolled over him. "I don't believe it," he said firmly. "They swore to me it was Bill Jones."

"They swore to Patcher it was Henry Smith. You can't even go to court with this, Frederick. A twelve-year-old would destroy the O'Connells' credibility in two minutes. Your whole case goes down the drain."

Frederick's eyes were wide and his face deathly pale. "Why would Patcher have got this affidavit? It must be a fraud. The man was a criminal, after all."

"Well, we don't know that he was. I expect so, but we have no proof. Now, why did he want that affidavit?" William leaned back in his chair with his hands behind his head. "It's an interesting question. I've given it some thought. My guess is that he was intending to blackmail

Chipper. Suppose Chipper succeeds in his claim to be Charles's son and come into the estate. Patcher turns up with his affidavit, spoiling Chipper's game. Caught that way, Chipper has to buy Patcher off. He might have to buy the O'Connells off as well, but that's not Patcher's concern. Chipper would have had to set him up for life. You have to admit, Frederick, this man Patcher had it thought through." Life, he was thinking, has its twists and turns; you had to take the long view.

Frederick was sitting stock-still. "Is there no out? Surely you don't want this, William."

"What I want is irrelevant, I'm afraid the fact that the boy had the gold sovereign all along is pretty convincing."

"But perhaps Patcher took it off the body, too." Frederick's hands were tightly clenched.

"He's had it for years. Chipper says that some of the gang members had seen it. They could be found if it went to court."

"But the ring. Surely Elizabeth must grasp that Chipper was lying about his mother's having the ring. And if he were lying about that, why is he not lying about everything else?"

William shook his head. "We can't prove that. The mother could have turned the ring over to Patcher for some purpose. Some scheme of their own that ended when she died. We're speculating. Why, if Patcher had taken the ring from the body, hadn't he sold it right away?"

Frederick stared out the window, his long, white face slack. Then he snapped his head back to William. "Perhaps

Elizabeth was in on it somehow. Why was she in touch with a man like Patcher?"

William shook his head. "I haven't the faintest idea, really. As we know, after Charles's body was found, she asked the Pinkerton men to find the boy who'd dragged it in. Patcher, of course. She wanted to know more about the circumstances of Charles's death. Where exactly had Patcher found him, and so forth. She kept up the relationship. I can't tell you why."

"You don't think she was cooking up something just to do me dirt?" Frederick said. His eyes narrowed. "Elizabeth never liked me, you know."

"No, I don't think that. Nor will any court."

Frederick looked sadly out of the window, not really seeing the ships cutting white wakes in the blue water. "Chipper's lying about the ring."

William shrugged. "Only Chipper knows, and I doubt that he's about to tell us. It doesn't matter, anyway. There's the sovereign. And the name—Chipper can be a nickname for Charles." He paused, looking thoughtful. "If I were of a sentimental turn of mind I might even believe that the mother was too proud to come to us after Charles died, but nonetheless hoped to make the connection." He rapped his fingers on the desk top. "Fortunately, I am not much given to sentiment."

Frederick looked down at his hand. "What do you suggest I do, William?"

"I suggest that you become a very loving cousin to Chipper Sibley, as he will be. I'm afraid that Elizabeth isn't pleased about your role in this, but in time Chipper may forgive. He doesn't seem an unreasonable boy. Rough and ill-educated, of course, but Elizabeth will have the rough edges smoothed off."

After Frederick left, William sat for a moment looking out the window and thinking. Perhaps it was for the best. Frederick lacked gumption, that was clear. Whatever you could say about Chipper, he didn't lack gumption, coming up there at great risk to himself to warn the house about the robbery. If the coachman hadn't fired when he had and driven the marauders off, the gang might have killed Chipper, too.

There was a great deal to do before they could go to Newport for the summer. Chipper had never seen such turmoil in his life. Huge trunks were being packed with more clothes than Chipper had known any human being to have. Silverware was being stored in vaults, other valuables locked in safes. There were tickets to be bought, letters to be written, calls to be made, summer uniforms for the servants got out of storage, the furniture in the house to be covered with sheets to prevent fading in the summer sun— oh, such a lot of turmoil.

However, there were certain advantages to the turmoil. Miss Sibley—or Aunt Elizabeth, as she was now—had insisted that Chipper start with a tutor immediately. The man came to the house for six hours a day, making Chipper's life miserable with fractions, Latin verb conjugations, the capitals of countries Chipper had never heard of before and didn't care if he ever heard of again. Miss Sibley—Aunt Elizabeth, rather—said he was far behind his cousins and must catch up. He was as smart as they were and must not run behind. However, with the turmoil, the lessons were frequently interrupted, and he found time to sit quietly by himself and wonder at how his life had changed.

He had not yet got used to the tight collars and chafing shoes that he was expected to wear. He was also not used to eating so much food as was provided for him—meat, oatmeal, eggs for breakfast; roast and gravy for dinner at noon; a "light" supper of something like baked beans and brown bread, with pickles, butter, relish. Aunt Elizabeth had told him that he wasn't required to eat everything on the table, but Chipper couldn't get out of the habit of eating everything available when he could.

Nor, as much as he liked living in the round room, had he yet got used to sleeping on a soft bed under linen sheets. Sometimes, just to get comfortable, he would get out of bed and lie down on the carpet, wrapped in a blanket.

In truth, at times he missed his old life with the Midnight Rats: missed sitting around the fire roasting potatoes and cracking jokes with Annie, Shad, and the rest of them. But he knew he couldn't go back to his old life. The police had caught up with the gang, dragging Pinch along, a few blocks down Fifth Avenue. They had dropped him and fled. Pinch had survived the wound but had gone off to the reformatory, and the gang had broken up. Or so the police had told William Hodge—now, of course, Cousin William.

So there was no Midnight Rats to go back to in any case. Someday, Chipper thought, he would try to find some of them, and perhaps even do something for them if he could. Sadly, he could not see them now, for they would assume he had double-crossed them to Patcher.

Chipper supposed he would get used to the stiff clothes and the soft bed. But although he had times when he missed the old days, in truth, most of the time he could not believe his luck. To be sure, there was so much to learn: not just fractions and Latin verbs, but how to hold a fork, how to eat soup, the names of all of his new cousins, as well as a great many other people Aunt Elizabeth knew, the right ways to introduce a lady to a gentleman, how to write a thank-you note, and so much more. Being rich was not quite as simple as he had supposed it was.

Moreover, he had reason to be uneasy about a couple of other things. For one, the cousins all seemed to believe that he had come up to the house that terrible night in order to warn them of the impending robbery. It was true, of course, that he had come to see that Aunt Elizabeth was not harmed. As for the rest of it, though, he had been responsible for letting them in—or would have been if Patcher had not interfered. He would explain this to Aunt Elizabeth one day soon so as to get it off his conscience. She would like it that he had come to protect her. As for the others, they could go on believing whatever they liked.

The question of the ring was more troubling. At times it seemed to him that he could remember seeing the ring back when he had been little; but he knew that in fact he had not. He also knew that people were suspicious about it. Cousin Frederick had said something to him a few days after the terrible night, something like, "I always assumed that somebody had taken the ring from Charles's body when it was found. Now we know it must have been Patcher."

Aunt Elizabeth had already said, "Chipper, be very careful of Frederick." So when Cousin Frederick had said that about Patcher taking the ring from Charles Sibley's body, Chipper had said, "I didn't know that. The way I remember it, Ma had it all along. Maybe she gave it to him or something."

Cousin Frederick had got a sour look on his face, as if he had eaten lemon, had said, "Possibly," and walked off.

In this respect, Chipper had been very lucky that the coachman and the stable boy had come running up *after* Patcher had admitted taking the ring. Not that any of it would have mattered, really. Everybody had seen right away that the sovereign was solid evidence. Chipper had, of course, shown it to Aunt Elizabeth as soon as the police had taken away poor Dick Patcher's body, and they had gone back into the house. She had got out a magnifying glass, and they had stood on the sofa side by side, comparing the coin in the picture with the coin in his hand. There wasn't any question about it anymore. Some day, Chipper thought, he would tell her the truth about the whole thing. Not now, certainly—she had had enough shocks for the time being. Not for a while, in all probability. But some day he would tell her.

Meanwhile, as Chipper was ruminating on all of this instead of doing fractions as he was supposed to be doing, Miss Sibley was upstairs on her sofa. In her head was a quiet dream of a mischievous boy letting a sailboat heel in the waters off Newport harbor until the foam was pouring in over the gunnels, threatening to tip the boat over.